MURDER
IN
HIGH PLACE

MURDER
IN
HIGH PLACE

R. B. Dominic

PUBLISHED FOR THE CRIME CLUB BY
DOUBLEDAY & COMPANY, INC.
GARDEN CITY, NEW YORK
1970

All of the characters in this book
are fictitious, and any resemblance
to actual persons, living or dead,
is purely coincidental.

Chapter 1

Washington, D.C. is the capital of the nation as well as one of the great centers of the free world. As a result, the business of official Washington involves both domestic matters and complicated international relationships. Either can be endlessly fascinating; either can be unbelievably dull. But on the whole, Washington agrees with the public at large: the international panorama may not always be more interesting and glamorous than the local scene, but it shares the glitter of Embassy Row.

In fact, from the Bureau of Fisheries and Hatcheries to the Congress of the United States, foreign parts and foreign policy exercise a heady appeal. Many a small-town politician rises through the political ranks on a platform of higher farm prices or lower interest rates only to discover, when he reaches Washington, that he has something of importance to say about tensions in the Middle East or land reform in Southeast Asia. He says it, sometimes on the floor of the House of Representatives, more often on the floor of the Senate, but always on television.

"Damned blabbermouth!" Congressman Eugene Valingham Oakes (R., S.Dak.) muttered as he straggled out of the chamber of the House of Representatives with Benton Safford (D., Ohio).

"I haven't said a word, Val," Safford protested.

"If you had," Oakes retorted testily, "it wouldn't be about churches in Poland. Not unless you've changed a lot, Ben."

The last speech of the day, mercifully cut short by the House's time limit, had been delivered by a member from Chicago, Illinois.

"I don't have many Poles in my district, Val," Ben Safford said fairly. The orator, Congressman Scycyzmk, was, after all, a fellow Democrat. Still, as Oakes irately left him, Ben Safford was obliged to admit that his old friend was justified. With major legislation logjammed before adjournment, Benton Safford, too, regretted the intrusion of religious squabbles in Warsaw and points east.

"Still, look at it this way," said Congressman Anthony Martinelli (D., R.I.) who was strolling along the corridor with him. "Across the way, that nutboy could talk for hours."

But they had reached Martinelli's office, so Ben Safford did not waste time by pointing out that, when a U. S. Senator takes flight into the lower reaches of political philosophy, he is usually the only one on the floor. House members are trapped by the very brevity of their allotted speech time. Instead, he steered his companion out of the stream of traffic and spoke earnestly about soybean prices.

"OK, OK!" said Tony cheerfully a few minutes later. This virtually assured the passage of Amendment II, dear to Safford's heart and dearer still to seven hundred of his constituents. "Where'd you go for the recess, Ben?"

Benton Safford had spent the Easter recess back home, in Newburg, Ohio. He looked down at his short, dapper companion. "You didn't spend the recess in Providence, Tony."

2

It was not a question. Congressman Martinelli was only fleetingly in his district.

"Ireland, Italy, and Israel," he said, shooting a dazzling cuff. "And a few other spots in between, but they're not for publication."

As he continued on toward his own office, Ben Safford grinned to himself. The congressmen who devoted themselves to weighty international issues came and went; the stayers, who included Tony Martinelli, as well as Val Oakes and Benton Safford, took care of the folks back home—as Oakes put it. It was simply that in Rhode Island, this necessitated Ireland, Italy and Israel.

Newburg, Ohio, which Ben had represented for nearly sixteen years, was a horse of a different color. Spectacular trips to distant places cut no ice in Newburg, unless these trips were taken in uniform. Safford, in Marine garb, had visited a satisfactory number of Pacific islands some years ago. Furthermore Newburg did not go in for fancy tailoring. Which was fortunate, since Ben Safford had a gift for making even new suits look rumpled.

No, what Newburg wanted and got from its congressman was close attention to its needs and desires. And despite outsiders, who kept voting Newburg the typical Midwest town and a rare piece of Americana, these needs went far beyond the price of soybeans. There were the factories out past Lincolnwood, worried about Japanese steel imports, union contracts and corporation taxes. There was Ed Daly, Democratic Committeeman, who worried about postmasterships and Federal Highway Programs. There was Newburg College, worried about AEC grants and the draft, as well as Newburg Savings and Loan, worried about the interest rate. And there were 34,765 men, women and children, worried about: a son at Fort Bragg, a job in the Veterans' Administration, a stray Social Security check, a disallowed tax deduction, a GPO publication or a new gun law.

3

All of this was enough to keep Congressman Benton Safford too busy to address the larger issues of our times. So, although it was late afternoon and Safford had spent the morning in committee and the afternoon on the floor, he was not planning to depart for his bachelor quarters at the Carlton Hotel but to put in two good hours at his correspondence. Declining several offers of refreshment, he made his way down the marbled corridor to his office and entered, encountering his secretary. But Madge Anderson was not seated at her desk. Instead, she was standing, head cocked, just outside the office of Douglas Travers, Safford's administrative assistant. Obviously Madge, an attractive and self-possessed young lady who ran the office with smiling efficiency, was trying to hear what was going on behind the closed door. Seeing him, she raised a finger to her lips.

Mystified, Safford suppressed the greeting he had been about to utter and did some listening on his own. The first voice he heard was his young assistant's basso.

". . . make an appointment for you."

"Don't give me that run-around," retorted a clear youthful soprano. "I came here to see my congressman and I'm staying until I do!"

The basso deepened into an incomprehensible rumble.

Safford approved. In spite of provocation, Doug Travers was controlling himself. Unfortunately this control seemed to exasperate his opponent.

"No, I'm not writing a letter. I'm sitting right here. The only way you'll get me out is to have the fuzz drag me out, bodily!"

"By fuzz, I suppose you mean the House Security Force," snapped Travers.

"Whatever you call your goon squad!"

Safford had heard enough to realize he could use a briefing. With a jerk of his head he indicated his own

4

inner office to Madge. When they were settled down behind closed doors, he demanded:

"Who is that in there with Travers?"

Madge was half-worried, half-amused.

"That is Mrs. Karen Kimball Jenks," she announced, rolling the words impressively.

The name seemed familiar. Quickly Safford ran down a mental list of his most pugnacious constituents.

"She sounds like a kid," he said as memory failed to stir.

"Mrs. Jenks is twenty-two—and was headline news a month ago."

Safford frowned. A good deal had happened in the last four weeks.

"Let me in on the joke, Madge," he said impatiently. "Is this some kind of student protest?"

"Not yet," said Madge brightly. "Although Mrs. Jenks tells me that she is a veteran of Chicago and knows how to deal with politicians."

"Oh yeah?" Ben grunted. "I thought the essence of that approach was to get together a mob of ten thousand."

"She seems to favor the one-woman blitzkrieg." Madge sighed. "I can see that I'd better start at the beginning."

"Good idea," said Safford.

She ignored him. "You recall that huge fuss in Nuevador last month?" she asked.

Safford got his pipe glowing. "Now listen, Madge. Just because I don't run around making speeches about the Alliance for Progress, you shouldn't assume that I don't read the newspapers." Yet, despite this dignified reproof, Safford could not recall details. Headlines about happenings in South America have almost no staying power. "Now, let's see. There was an incident, wasn't there? Yes, I remember. An American was accused of insulting the President of the Republic . . ."

"And the Archbishop," Madge added rather gaily.

5

Safford eyed her. "Then there were anti-American riots and the usual. Right?"

"Roughly," said Madge, still obscurely amused. "I just looked up the details for you."

Safford held his ground despite these ominous words. "Before you tell me more than I want to know about a second-rate, corrupt banana republic, just tell me two things. Does this Mrs. Jenkins enter into it? More to the point, is she a constituent of mine?"

"I hate to tell you, but it's yes to both," Madge replied. "And it's Mrs. Karen *Jenks*. Shall I go on?" She took a deep breath. "Well, four weeks ago, there was a Mass for the Republic—that's an annual holiday down in Nuevador. The President, the Foreign Colony and other dignitaries were all there. Suddenly a young American woman managed to slip past the Guardia Civile and rushed into the crowded basilica—"

"Some guards," Safford murmured derisively, but Madge continued:

"She interrupted the sacred services, shouted insults at all concerned and threw anti-Nuevadorian pamphlets around. As you can imagine, she created an uproar."

"During which, she somehow escaped," Ben added. Details, many of them unattractive, were returning to him. "But they produced photographs, didn't they? Supporting the official protests?"

"Yes, indeed," said Madge sweetly. "They confirmed the story of all the witnesses—that, in addition to insulting the State and the Church, this young woman was virtually naked. That was an insult to simple Nuevadorian decency and honor."

Thinking deeply, Ben decided to ignore Nuevadorian notions of decency and honor. "I've never pretended to understand women, Madge. Particularly young women who make public protests. But will you tell me why she should take her clothes off?"

6

But Madge Anderson was not taken in. "Mr. Congressman, you're not old enough for this venerable approach to women."

"Still, I'm getting there, thank God," he said feelingly. Safford was not yet fifty, but he had no intention of dragging boyishness with him to the grave like so many of his colleagues.

Madge persevered. "At any rate, the important thing is that, as a result of the publicity, there were serious anti-American riots. Several people were killed. You see, the photographs identified the woman as this young Sears Scholar . . ."

"Mrs. Jenks," said Safford. "Who is now sitting in Travers' office. Tell me, does she have her clothes on?"

"Some," said Madge serenely.

Startled, Safford looked up. "But what does she want?"

Enunciating clearly, Madge said:

"She wants her congressman to help her prove that the photographs are, in her words, stinking fakes. She wants her congressman to get those lousy rats—that's the Nuevadorian government—to apologize and invite her back to Nuevador. She wants her congressman to get off his ass and do something about those morons in the State Department. She wants . . ."

Weakly, Safford raised a hand. "All right, I've got the picture. Tell me one more thing. Is she a folksinger or something?"

Rising gracefully, Madge said, "Oh no, sir. She's doing research for a doctorate in cultural anthropology."

"Oh, my God!"

"Just wait," said Madge cheerfully. "Should I tell her and Doug to come in? He's had quite a dose."

There was, unfortunately, only one answer.

Karen Jenks, who appeared a few minutes later trailed by Douglas Travers, was fully clothed. Even so, she reminded Safford of some tawny beast of prey, poised to strike. Her

7

sleek curtains of silver-blond hair, her level blue eyes ringed with artful eye shadow, were undeniably results of civilization. But the fluid ease of her movements and the stormy passion of her face suggested a wilder arena than a congressman's office.

Chin up, she paused on the threshold.

After one glance at Doug, Safford decided to dispense with niceties.

"Mrs. Jenks? I'm Ben Safford . . ."

Doug Travers was rigid, but he was ready to carry on. Grimly, he began: "Mrs. Jenks, this is Congressman Safford . . ."

Unfortunately, they collided.

Coolly inspecting Safford, Mrs. Jenks flung herself into a chair with a flourish of attractive long legs. "I hope this means we're finally getting down to business."

"Tell me," said Benton Safford after a pause during which Douglas Travers took a deep breath, "what the business is." He then sat and waited. Mrs. Jenks, who spoke in spasmodic little rushes, looked at him suspiciously.

"Gladly. For the past two weeks I've been trying to tell someone. I've tried to tell the Sears Foundation, I've tried to tell TASA, I've tried to tell the State Department. And all I've gotten is one solid brush-off. And he"—she indicated Travers—"has been trying to carry on the good work."

Doug Travers ignored the attack. "Mrs. Jenks," he said sarcastically, "doesn't feel that her problem is getting enough attention in Washington."

"Problem!" the girl exploded. She started digging into a huge pouch made of native leather with two heavy silver initials. "Will you look at this!"

Safford reached out to examine the newspaper clippings that Mrs. Jenks hurled across the desk. There were two pictures and a good deal of Spanish print. Even in reproduction, they had the brutal clarity of spotlights breaching the darkness. Against a confused background of faces, raised arms and shadows blazed a white beacon, a magnificent young body holding high a clutch of papers. She was, as Madge had said, virtually naked. A wild swirl of long hair caught the light. In the second picture, only a part of the girl appeared. It was a close-up that showed long legs—and the flag they were kicking.

Involuntarily, Safford glanced at his visitor.

"Yes!" she snarled with a savagery that almost made him jump. "Yes, that's me! No, I am not naked. I'm wearing a bikini, like millions of other people!"

"All right," Safford said hurriedly. "All right, Mrs. Jenks. I don't suppose you can tell me why you were wearing a bikini in a cathedral . . ."

"But I wasn't!" she wailed, suddenly sounding ten years younger. "That's the point! I've never been in that antiquated heap in my life!"

"I thought you just said . . ."

"That's what I've been trying to get through Jumbo's head here! It's a fake! It's a frame-up!"

Doug Travers replied to the wail, not to the insult. "If you'd just calm down and be reas—"

"Oh, shut up!"

Both voices started to rise.

"Quiet!" Safford bellowed.

A quivering silence enveloped the office. Firmly Congressman Safford seized the initiative.

"Obviously we're not going to get anywhere this way. Mrs. Jenks, you had better tell me the whole story. As calmly as you can, please."

Shooting a contemptuous look toward Travers, she muttered ungraciously, "All right. Well . . ."

Mrs. Jenks' narrative was not exactly calm. Yet she was surprisingly well organized and concise.

Karen Kimball Jenks, aged twenty-two, divorced and the mother of a fourteen-month-old infant . . .

"God almighty!" Douglas Travers exploded.

9

"What do you want, patty-cake?" she spat back.

"Could you just push on to the essentials," said Safford wearily. Travers and Mrs. Jenks had reached surprisingly intimate, if bad, terms during a short interview, he reflected. Of course, those pictures were icebreakers if ever he saw any.

The baby was now being cared for by Karen's mother in Newburg. ("No, we're not old-timers. Dad just transferred there three years ago from Chicago. I suppose you only get moving for old-timers. Oh, all right . . .") This left Karen free to resume her education. ("Of course I was in school while I was married. You can't stay in bed all day, you know!") She had graduated from Radcliffe (Travers snorted but subsided at a look from Safford) and had decided to do graduate work. She was then fortunate enough to win a Sears Foundation scholarship which made field work possible. In Nuevador.

"Let's stop right here," said Safford. "Did you at that time have any connection with Nuevador or Nuevadorians?"

Mrs. Jenks, now smoking with the same suppressed urgency that marked her speech, looked at him with flashing eyes. "At least you keep your eye on essentials," she said with something like approval. "Not like Jack Armstrong, All-American Boy, here."

"Mrs. Jenks," Ben said, "are there any temptations you resist?"

It was a half-smile, with only one corner of the mouth curling up. "None that I can think of," she said.

"I was afraid of that," said Ben. "Well, back to Nuevador . . ."

But no, Karen Jenks had had no connection at all with Nuevador.

"I see," said Safford. "And then . . . once you got there?"

Once Karen Jenks reached Nuevador, she had moved into the teeming, squalid slums that ring the capital city,

Montecigalpa, like fetid sores. Armed with tape recorder, typewriter, and reference works she began her research among the poor.

"Did you get interested in their politics?" Ben asked sharply, interrupting a description of sanitary facilities.

She looked at him with blank hostility. "I went to Nuevador to do my work."

Ben was nettled. "Look, Mrs. Jenks. I didn't ask if you were running guns. I asked if you got interested—in a simple human sense. After all, every time you criticize the establishment, you're involved in politics."

She flared into arrogance. "That's a stupid way to put it."

"Only," Ben pointed out, "because you didn't say it yourself. Now think!"

"Of course I got interested in their politics, if that's what you want to call it. I saw those greasy policemen shaking down the prostitutes just a block from where I lived! I saw the customs collectors down at the docks, looking the other way when illegal Cadillacs were imported by some general! A dirty little bastard from the Ministry of Education propositioned me, then got so ugly I had to use my knee! Just two blocks from the President's Palace I saw American aid on sale—aid that was supposed to go up to the Indians in the mountains! I saw filthy, corrupt excuses for human beings. You do, you know, if you are trying to learn about how the poor live! And if you call that politics —sure! I saw Nuevadorian politics!"

At this moment, Ben Safford began to believe Karen Kimball Jenks. If he had heard an exposé of the shattering weakness of Nuevador's new government, or an indictment of the reactionary opposition—well, he might have wondered. Even a catalog of mistakes made by the United States— which would have taken time—would not have surprised him. But if Karen Jenks had any political sophistication at all, it was well hidden.

Nor did she strike him as a girl to pretend. On the contrary, there was a certain ruthless simplicity about her.

"And I suppose, if you really wanted to dance naked in their cathedral, you would—and be damned to everyone," he murmured aloud.

"Look," she said, hoarse with intensity. "I did not dance in that damned cathedral. You don't understand. There I was, doing my work, minding my own business. I didn't even know they were having a holiday. And the next morning I woke up and saw those things in the paper!"

She prodded the news cuttings with her forefinger.

"I couldn't believe my eyes! I was so shook up it took me days to figure out what some bastard had done."

"Yes," urged Safford, caught in spite of himself by the possibilities of her story. "And what was that?"

"I'll show you." Once again she dived into the pouch. This time it was not newsprint that she produced, but several glossy little snapshots. "Look! Pictures of me on the beach at Nuevador. You can see for yourself. This is the one they superimposed on that cathedral picture. That's why the lighting is so sharp."

Interestedly Ben studied the two pictures. Both Madge and Doug had advanced to the desk and were bending over his shoulder. The beach photo had been taken in bright sunlight. It showed Karen, in the famous bikini, leaping for a beach ball. The cathedral photograph showed her in an identical pose. And now that it had been brought to his attention, Safford realized that the bright light bathing the figure in the dimly lit cathedral was suspicious.

"There were quite a lot of pictures of the cathedral incident, as I recall," he said thoughtfully. "Did they all correspond to snapshots of yours?"

"You bet they did," Karen said triumphantly. "All the ones that showed my face, that is. But I can tell you something else. That's why I brought the other cutting along.

You see those legs kicking that flag—well, they're not my legs. Take a look."

Invitingly, she stretched out her own shapely limbs. This produced kindly interest from Madge, disapproval from Doug Travers and a critical examination from Safford.

"I don't see how you can say that," he said finally. "If the other pictures have been superimposed I'm willing to take your word for it, but I don't see how you can prove anything about this shot of legs."

"My scar," she said impatiently, "my scar."

And then Safford saw. Mrs. Jenks' legs were not only beautifully formed, they were beautifully tanned. They were a rich even bronze everywhere except on her left ankle where a narrow stripe of scar tissue remained white. Quickly he turned to the second cutting. The flag kicker, whoever she had been, possessed a totally unblemished left ankle.

"Tell me, Mrs. Jenks," he said at length, "these are all very strong points that you're making. Why didn't you make any of them at the time?"

All the girl's resentment returned in a rush.

"My God, you don't think anybody listened to my side of things, do you? I was given such a bum's rush out of Nuevador, I didn't have time to think, I didn't have time to do anything. I had my hands full trying to protect my records. They tried to make me leave them behind. I told them I'd kick and fight every inch of the way to the airport. They were just going to dump me on the first plane out."

Safford could readily believe Mrs. Jenks' description of her resistance. It was, after all, merely a variant on her earlier stand with Doug Travers. But he thought he saw something else, too.

"You were lucky you managed to hang on to your belongings," he observed. "Otherwise you wouldn't have these beach snapshots."

"Lucky!" She was almost spitting in rage. "Don't you see

13

where this leaves me? Somebody doctored a picture of me. Then they used it to put pressure on the Embassy! And they got the Sears Foundation to withdraw my grant! I've done over eight months' work in Montecigalpa—and it's all going to be wasted if I can't go back and finish it! That's all I want to do! This just isn't fair!"

Mrs. Jenks saw nothing incongruous in this plaint.

"It isn't fair," Safford agreed. "Tell me, have you asked yourself why all of this should have happened?"

Again that blank hostile gaze. No, Safford told himself, Karen Jenks was too preoccupied with what she wanted to concern herself with other questions. She had the single-mindedness of a child; she wanted to go back to Nuevador and finish her work. And it wasn't fair that something should stand in her way.

The fact that it was, according to her account, a deliberate attempt at international scandal—well, that didn't occur to her. He began to feel mildly curious about the unknown Mrs. Kimball, back in Newburg, who not only had raised Karen but was now coping with a fourteen-month-old infant while her daughter pursued tribal lore in South America. Absently he drew some question marks on a scratch pad.

"Well?" Karen Jenks demanded.

"Let me make some inquiries, Mrs. Jenks," Safford began.

"Inquiries? What good will inquiries do? You've got to go to the State Department and make them protest to these . . ."

Again Safford raised his hand. "Hold it, Mrs. Jenks. You may as well get a few things straight. First, I cannot drop my other responsibilities to devote myself to your interest full-time. Second, I very much doubt that we can get the U. S. Navy to send a destroyer. So it's got to be inquiries. I will, I promise you, make them. If you have been victimized, well, we'll try to do what we can. More I cannot promise—and you would be unreasonable to expect it."

Another one of her passionate silences. Then, abruptly, she said, "All right. That's fair enough. For now."

Safford was too old a hand to reveal any emotion, or amusement. Instead he rose to escort her to the hall.

"But don't expect me to sit still," she said. "I'm going to do what I can."

This threat reached Douglas Travers, ostensibly conferring with Madge Anderson.

"I don't suppose," Safford said genially, "that there is any use urging you to be discreet?"

For the first time in their interview, Karen Jenks smiled radiantly.

"Nobody else has found it any use," she said.

"I didn't think so," Safford murmured. "Now, we have your current address, do we . . ."

They did. A minute later, and Congressman Safford and his staff were watching Mrs. Jenks swing jauntily out of the office.

"Just another one of those sweet old-fashioned girls you rear in Newburg," said Madge with a ripple of laughter. She came from San Francisco.

Douglas Travers snorted angrily. "Girl, hell! She's married, divorced and a mother. She's been in jail in Chicago and kicked out of a foreign country. If she's not grown up now, it's time she was."

"I think that's the wave of the future," said Safford with a grin as he moved back toward his office. "Still, that smile makes quite a difference, doesn't it?"

He had not moved out of earshot, though, before he heard Travers' reply.

"Not enough, it doesn't. Not by a long shot!"

Chapter 2

Karen Kimball Jenks had swept into Congressman Ben Safford's life like a whirlwind. It soon became obvious that she was not going to sweep out of it with anything like the same speed.

"We might as well do what we can," Ben announced. "Do you want to start with the Sears Foundation, Madge?"

With that, Ben put Mrs. Jenks from his mind and went into his own office. There he spent a productive hour, polishing some remarks he was scheduled to make to a group of visiting firemen. When he finished, he went to the doorway.

"Madge, you won't forget to try the Sears Foundation, will you? I'd like to get this Jenks girl off our necks—" He broke off, belatedly absorbing Madge's scowl, as well as the notebooks spread open beside her, the memos she had scribbled to herself, and the fact that she was on the phone.

"What was that extension number?" she was saying with ice in her voice. "Yes, will you please transfer me . . . yes . . ." Cupping a hand over the phone, she said, "I have

16

been getting the run-around to end all—hello? I am calling on behalf of Congressman Safford, of Ohio, in connection with a Mrs. Jenks—J-E-N-K-S . . . No? Well, do you know who *does* know anything about it? . . . Yes, I'll wait . . ."

Just then, Doug Travers came into the office, clutching a scrap of paper. "Got it," he told Madge. "Lou says the guy you want is Quentin Fels." He read from his notes. "He's Director of Overseas Grants. Extension 8876."

Unceremoniously Madge downed the receiver, waited one minute, then started dialing again.

Now, John Q. Public may get the run-around from large institutions in Washington, D.C. Normally, congressmen do not. Ben narrowed his eyes thoughtfully, while he and Doug heard Madge get Quentin Fels' office, then his secretary. Mr. Fels was out. Mr. Fels was busy. Mr. Fels would call back.

"I am afraid that this is very urgent," said Madge coldly. "Congressman Safford is waiting."

Despite the determined roadblocking of the Sears Foundation, Mr. Fels himself was smooth and cooperative when he was finally run to ground some five minutes later.

"I wish I could help you, Congressman," he said weightily, "but I don't quite see how this is a problem of the Sears Foundation."

Ben replied that the Sears Foundation had sent Karen Jenks to Nuevador, and the Sears Foundation had recalled Karen Jenks. Whose problem was it?

"Oh, I don't think it's quite accurate to say that we recalled her," the phone interrupted. "After all, we are an American institution. When the government tells us that one of our people overseas has become *persona non grata,* why, the Sears Foundation has no option but to cooperate with the State Department."

Ben was taking an unreasonable dislike to the fluent Mr. Fels. "The State Department asked you to recall her? Exactly who, in the State Department?"

This question did not please Fels. "I did not say things were done that directly," he protested. "Of course, there is no doubt that the State Department would have asked us to act, if we had delayed."

For the first time, Ben Safford felt real sympathy for Karen Jenks. "Mr. Fels, are you saying that your organization recalled Mrs. Jenks simply because you expected somebody to ask you to do so?"

Mr. Fels did not like this way of putting it. For the first time in their exchange, he was really spontaneous. "Good God, no!" he exclaimed. Then, more guardedly, he went on: "Let me assure you, Mr. Congressman, that Mrs. Jenks' recall was requested by a government agency. In view of the worldwide publicity caused by the whole unfortunate incident, the request was granted. We here at the Sears Foundation considered the whole matter very carefully. And I can assure you that no personal censure of Mrs. Jenks was implied. After all, we chose her for this research grant from a good many candidates. We've told Mrs. Jenks that we are willing to help her continue her work—here at home. But she is young, and occasionally young people are irresponsible. We've had a good deal of experience at the Sears Foundation . . ."

Mr. Fels broke off for a practiced indulgent chuckle. This gave Ben the opportunity he had been waiting for.

"That won't do," he said bluntly. "Mrs. Jenks is not attacking the recall in itself as unreasonable." Ben was lying and he knew it; Karen Jenks was capable of attacking anything and everything. "She does feel entitled to a hearing to prove that she was innocent of this alleged misconduct. And, speaking as her congressman, I must say that I agree."

This none-too-subtle nudge registered. The Sears Foundation had many good reasons to try to keep U. S. Congressmen sweet.

"Innocent!" Fels was outraged. "That picture was published all over the world."

Ben pressed on. "We may have to examine that picture more closely. But the point remains, Mrs. Jenks should have an opportunity to confront the people responsible for her recall. And you say that the Sears Foundation was not."

Fels was openly peevish. "A hearing simply means raking up all that publicity—"

"Mr. Fels," Safford cut in. "I will be able to learn what U.S. agency acted to recall Mrs. Jenks. If you don't want to cooperate . . ."

Mr. Fels retreated. "Very well," he snapped. "It was TASA—Technical Assistance to South America. The man you want," he amplified bitterly, "is Howard Creighton. He's head of their Pacific Area desk."

Ben extracted a telephone number before hanging up and facing Doug Travers who had been an interested listener. "You know, Doug, I'm beginning to get a strange feeling . . ."

Travers waited for him to go on but he fell silent. One thing a congressman learns or he doesn't go on being a congressman long—the smell of a political mess.

Ben was beginning to detect the old familiar aroma. "Let's see about this Creighton, Madge."

Madge squared her shoulders. But TASA was not the Sears Foundation. With its usual open-sesame effect, Safford's name and office got past secretaries and executive assistants. Almost immediately he had Mr. Howard Creighton on the line.

Creighton was not as evasive as Quentin Fels. "Karen Jenks? Sure, I asked the Sears people to pull her out. After that caper in the cathedral. Hell, Nuevador is a tinderbox. I didn't want some American kid lighting the fuse."

"I see," said Ben.

Creighton misinterpreted this. "Don't get me wrong, Mr.

Congressman. The Embassy agreed with me fully. If I hadn't acted, they would have."

Carefully, Ben repeated his point about looking into the justice of the facts.

Howard Creighton did not disguise his reaction. "God, that's all we need, now," he groaned. "Still—look, Congressman, you must see our position here at TASA. Now that we've got the newspapers shut up about Karen Jenks and the Nuevadorians, the last thing we want is more publicity."

Ben said that he did not want publicity either. He did not comment on what Karen Jenks wanted.

"Good," said Creighton. "Now if your girl just wants to have another tantrum—well, I'm not going to let TASA oblige her. Hell, she's caused us enough trouble. But on the other hand, if she's really had a raw deal—well, I suppose something should be done. I'll be frank with you. I hope that's not the case—but I'll listen, so long as it's in private."

"Fair enough," said Safford.

Howard Creighton was businesslike. "OK," he said. "Phil Barnes and I can set up a meeting," he said, clearly making notes. "I think we'd better notify the Nuevadorian Embassy so they can send somebody if they want. Otherwise they'll go up in smoke and we'll have another crisis on our hands."

Ben said he was willing to go along with that.

"Well, I was wrong," he said to Doug after Creighton rang off some minutes later. "I think we're going to be able to handle this pretty well. Creighton, at least, is trying to play ball."

Now, just why did Doug Travers look so unconvinced, Ben ruminated as he returned to his desk and weightier affairs.

He found out speedily enough.

First, there was Karen Jenks. She was contemptuous to

learn that the best her congressman could do was produce a hearing.

"I know what they have in mind over at TASA," the phone scoffed. "They think this is going to be a nice face-saving session where they congratulate themselves on getting rid of a troublemaker."

This was close enough to the truth to silence Safford.

"Well, it won't work," Mrs. Jenks promised darkly. "I've already had an earful from that sanctimonious little bastard, Barnes. And Creighton is just another bureaucrat. Do you think anybody at TASA, or the Sears Foundation, cares about the life of a Nuevadorian peasant—"

"No," Ben broke in to say, "and if you have any brains at all, you won't raise the subject. Concentrate on that photograph. Bring along plenty of copies. If we can prove it was doctored, you'll have it made."

This earned him a lecture on surrendering principle for profit. Curtly, Ben informed Mrs. Jenks that he would expect to see her tomorrow morning at ten-thirty in Room 1208 of the Sears Building.

Within seconds, there was another protest. But this was official, and it came from the State Department. Fortunately, an acquaintance delivered it.

"Ben, what's all this about Señora Montoya attending some closed session about the Jenks girl?"

Regretfully, Ben looked at the work piled high on his desk. He was beginning to feel that it would be a long time before he could get to it.

"What's the trouble, Carl?" he asked cautiously.

Carl Zimmerman was a sensible man in his mid-forties whom Ben had met during some congressional investigations. He and a surprisingly youthful wife had been pleasures to encounter on Ben's modest social round. Both Zimmermans were credits to the State Department and, like most of its credits, they periodically talked about leaving. But Carl Zimmerman was the son of diplomatic parents; Willa was the daughter of missionaries. Two family traditions of service—as well as two sons bright enough to finance their own education—kept Carl Zimmerman in the Department of State, where he had now risen to be second man on the South American desk.

"Creighton should have his head examined," Zimmerman was saying undiplomatically. "This won't do. If it turns out to be a whitewash for the girl—and I suppose that's what you have in mind—"

"Now, hold everything," Ben said. "First of all, whitewash isn't the best way to put it—when we're just asking for an honest inquiry."

Zimmerman said something about sleeping dogs.

"Also," Safford went on, "you don't know how fair I'm being about all this. If you've met Karen Jenks, you know that all my natural instincts are to let her sink or swim. But I can't let you people push my constituents around, Carl. Tell me, what's up with the Nuevadorian Embassy?"

Zimmerman was an even-tempered man. "I suppose you're right," he said. "There's got to be some sort of inquiry. But Ben, it's important that we treat it as a purely American deal—or else we get complete representation from the Nuevadorians. Not just Señora Montoya."

Ben registered Zimmerman's emphatic words. He just did not understand them. He said so.

Zimmerman sighed. "You know, I spend so much time with these Nuevadorians that I forget that everybody else isn't knee-deep in details."

Ben had already put in a full day. He was in no mood for State Department analysis, even from Carl Zimmerman. Let Nuevadorians take care of Nuevador. All he wanted was a briefing on the situation as it affected Karen Jenks.

"Oh God," said Zimmerman. "Well, you know they threw out the General and have a new reform government in Nuevador?"

Ben said that he didn't see how the General, his blonde,

22

his Swiss bank account and his present villa on the Riviera had anything to do with current events.

"That's where you're wrong," said Zimmerman cheerfully. "General Vallon is the key to the whole thing. This new reform government is pretty good, but it's weak. All over Nuevador there are power struggles—the old Vallonistas versus the new reformers. Well, the Nuevadorian Embassy is half and half—and this lunatic Creighton called up their cultural attaché who is the real old guard. So, I got a hot call from one of the reformers. Is the U.S. subverting their government? Is the State Department encouraging the old aristocrats who are dying to get back into power? Is . . ."

"Fine, fine," said Ben.

Tomorrow's meeting was now expanded to include Carl Zimmerman and two Nuevadorians: one a member of the hereditary ruling class, the other an impassioned supporter of the reform government.

He had been wrong, Ben decided, to mistrust that sense of smell. He had started by trying to get the Sears Foundation to listen to Karen Jenks. This had plunged him into the world of Latin American aid, internecine Nuevadorian politics and, he suspected, trouble between TASA and the State Department. What should have been an informal discussion with Quentin Fels was turning into a summit conference of four or five great powers. And despite the stress put on privacy by almost everybody, news of this meeting would certainly leak to the Washington press corps, creating further problems.

But even a sensitive nose can do only so much. Ben didn't like the whiffs he was getting, but by no stretch of the imagination did he foresee just exactly what lay in store for him.

Ten forty-five the following morning began it.

Without enthusiasm, Ben set off for the Sears Building on Connecticut Avenue, instead of Capitol Hill. It was a nice spring day, but Ben had a feeling that it was not going to be one for long. He clambered out of the taxi, proceeded into a busy lobby, and secured directions to the elevator. Room 1208, he discovered without surprise, looked like a successful cocktail party.

People—most of them unknown to Ben—filled the room.

With an inward sigh, he advanced on Carl Zimmerman who was flanked by two obvious foreigners. One was a woman of striking beauty, with the traditional raven hair and camelia skin; the other was a hawk-faced man of early middle age.

Just then, two things happened.

A thick energetic man with a shock of coarse blond hair materialized at Ben's side. He was introducing himself as Howard Creighton, of TASA, when he was rudely interrupted. The door was flung open unceremoniously. A slim, graying man stared at the gathering. For a moment, he could not speak. Then:

"My God! Didn't you hear anything? Philip Barnes is dead on the sidewalk! They think—they're saying he must have come out of this window!"

Chapter 3

Room 1208 was stupefied.

"He must have jumped out of this window, or the one next door." The messenger's excitement abruptly yielded to nausea. He gulped suspiciously and sank into a chair. "My God, he must have broken every bone in his body."

Ben Safford, who was trying to recall where he had heard the name "Philip Barnes," thought he recognized the speaker's voice. Someone from the crowd confirmed this: the man sagging in the chair was Quentin Fels, Director of Overseas Grants of the Sears Foundation. As Ben, and everybody else, stared at him, he raised his head: "Oh, this is terrible."

Howard Creighton shook free of shock and pushed his way to Fels' side. "Phil?" he said incredulously. "Phil killed himself? Are you sure?"

Carl Zimmerman had moved to the window. "Good God, Creighton, he's right. There's a big crowd down there."

The woman with raven hair said something in Spanish. As if released, the others broke into speech. Safford, it appeared, was the only one present who did not know who Philip Barnes was.

"I don't understand it," Howard Creighton was saying more to himself than to anyone else. "Phil! Of all people!"

Quentin Fels was struggling to regain his composure. Carl Zimmerman remained rooted to the spot by the window. Outside, the wail of sirens signaled the arrival of authorities.

"I'd better get down there," said Creighton, striding toward the door.

"Hold on," said Quentin Fels surprisingly. "I'll go with you."

Quite suddenly, the excitement outside the Sears Building, of alarms and red lights, of police and ambulances, was communicated indoors. There seemed to be a mass rushing through the corridors, with voices calling, shouting, asking. Minutes after Creighton and Fels hurried away, a uniformed officer appeared in the doorway.

"You people stay right here!" he said firmly.

"Officer, just a minute," Carl Zimmerman began, but the policeman had moved on to deliver the same message to other offices along the hallway.

"It is to be supposed," said the thin, sharp-faced man from the Nuevadorian Embassy, "that Mr. Fels was quite correct. That Mr. Barnes chose to jump from a window near this one." He studied the old-fashioned window frame thoughtfully.

"Just exactly who was Barnes?" Safford asked. The policeman's message suggested that he was going to be forced to remain in the Sears Building longer than he had expected. He did not intend to remain in a fog.

But this question jogged State Department instincts in Carl Zimmerman. Hurriedly, he embarked upon a round of introductions. Most of the round was lost on Safford who took several moments to absorb the impact of Señora Luisa Montoya. Here, it seemed, was Nuevador's cultural attaché. But Señora Montoya was a woman who would never need the prestige of her country or her high office to distinguish her. Quite apart from her great natural beauty, she was the glowing product of money and privilege. In her mid-thirties, she was at the peak of her physical attractions, aided by magnificent grooming and a superbly trained social manner. Without the slightest departure from decorum, Luisa Montoya exuded sexuality in a manner suggesting years of practice.

Safford recognized big guns when they were planted under his nose. No matter what her title, Señora Montoya was not in the United States to represent any reform government. She was born to represent power, and Ben was willing to bet that today this meant a watching brief for Nuevador's great landlords, the rich and the mighty who still dreamed of the restoration of the old regime. No wonder Carl Zimmerman was concerned about the lady. Interestedly, Ben turned to survey the man who must be present as her counterbalance.

There was no aura of privilege about Dr. Manuel Olivera. He was an economic counselor at the Embassy, a man with a dark intellectual face and nervous eyes. An untidy ash hanging from a crumpled cigarette imperiled an already untidy suit. He took up Safford's question and gave it an unexpected answer.

"Mr. Barnes," he said almost bitterly, "Mr. Barnes did not strike one as the man for defenestration."

Zimmerman leaped into the conversation.

"He was Howard Creighton's assistant at TASA," he explained.

Olivera supplemented this information. "Mr. Barnes was the TASA economic specialist for Nuevador. In effect, he supervised our technical aid from the United States."

"Nuevador's only technical aid," Señora Montoya said with a wealth of meaning.

Distractedly Zimmerman intervened again. "Barnes was

How's follow-up man, Mr. Congressman. He's in charge—
or he was in charge—of TASA shipments."

"An important position," said Dr. Olivera harshly. "But
much as I deplore this tragedy, I must remark that your
young policeman is going beyond the bounds of protocol in
demanding that I remain here. There is such a thing as
diplomatic immunity."

Señora Montoya took up the challenge immediately. "Dr.
Olivera, this is not the correct time for such legalism. The
policeman can have had no idea who you are—or indeed
who I am, for that matter. It would be discourteous for us
to refuse our assistance in the presence of such a tragedy.
After all, Mr. Barnes represented an agency that, thanks to
the generosity of the American people, supplies valuable
technical aid to Nuevador. I am sure that the Ambassador
would agree with me."

A silent battle of wills ensued. Señora Montoya emerged
the victor.

"Very well," said Dr. Olivera, turning aside with a shrug.
"We shall remain to render assistance, although I find it
difficult to understand how we can be of any help."

Carl Zimmerman and Señora Montoya relaxed too soon.
Dr. Olivera had reserved his bombshell for the room at
large.

With a sudden gleam of white teeth, he delivered his
final comment:

"Surprising is it not? We start with *l'affaire Jenks*, and
end with Mr. Barnes hurling himself from a window."

The implications of this shook Carl Zimmerman. Señora
Montoya disassociated herself from the sentiment with a
controlled gesture of distaste. But Ben Safford was reminded that Karen Kimball Jenks, and her problems, had
momentarily slipped his mind.

"I don't see any connection," Zimmerman began.

Just then Howard Creighton and Quentin Fels hurried
back into the room.

"Good heavens! Good heavens!" said Fels who had revived.

Creighton was pinched around the nostrils.

"What is it?" Zimmerman cried.

"It's murder," said Creighton dully.

The policeman at his heels did not contradict him.

Philip Barnes had certainly exited from the Sears Building via a window in or near Room 1208. But it did not take lengthy study to determine one other fact. The young intern from George Washington Hospital put it succinctly as he isolated one injury.

"He didn't get *that* from jumping out of a window." *That* was the portion of Barnes' skull not flattened by the fall; it was also a wound of unmistakably lethal proportions. Philip Barnes had been hit over the head with a heavy object before his fall. The fall itself had produced quite different injuries. This was enough for the police who swiftly sealed off the Sears Building.

If news that Philip Barnes was dead had startled Room 1208, the word *murder* stunned it.

Even an hour later, Howard Creighton's normal ruddiness was an ashy pallor. "Murder?"

"That's right," said Captain Rigsby who had taken charge. "Pretty clear he was dead or dying when he went out that window. Now then, what can you tell me . . ."

"Murder!" Carl Zimmerman exclaimed. "I can't believe it."

Dr. Olivera kindled another one of his rank cigarettes. "Why not? Myself, I find murder easier to accept than suicide."

"Dr. Olivera!" said Señora Montoya in sharp reproof.

To all appearances, Captain Rigsby was attending to the dispatch of subordinates or, alternatively, listening to the reports flowing into Room 1208. But Safford was sure that he was also registering the acrimonious atmosphere. Even

29

during the listless exchanges before the arrival of the police, Ben Safford had been struck by brittle crosscurrents he did not fully understand. His companions, of course, had been personally involved with Philip Barnes. Yet Safford was beginning to sense something else in the air. Suddenly he did not like the way things were shaping.

His reflections were interrupted. Quentin Fels recalled his responsibility as an official of the Sears Foundation.

"Of course, Captain, everything I can do to help. Although I find it impossible to credit this theory. It is most unlikely that anyone here at Sears had anything to do with this frightful event."

Captain Rigsby was not noticeably interested in Fels' opinions. "Fine. Now first, what can you tell me about the setup here?"

The Sears Building on Connecticut Avenue was really a normal business building with the top seven floors occupied by the administrative machinery of the Sears Foundation. Since the Foundation financed million-dollar projects throughout the world, this apparatus was large.

"Do you have any security guards checking visitors?" asked one of Rigsby's aides.

Fels pursed his lips. "We are not a government agency," he said waspishly. More to the point, the commercial tenants on the remaining floors of the Sears Building, who included real estate agencies and management consultants, would not tolerate security procedures in the lobby.

"Furthermore," said Fels, "we're a very busy place. Visitors from all over. Meetings . . ."

"Were you people having a meeting here today?" Rigsby asked.

Howard Creighton cleared his throat and shot a look at Benton Safford. "More of an informal discussion, Captain."

Rigsby accepted the amendment. "And Barnes was due at this meeting?"

"He was certainly planning to attend," said Creighton unhappily.

Captain Rigsby did not sound unhappy. On the contrary, there was a cheerful note in his voice. "Now we're getting somewhere. Let's go back to the beginning."

It took time but finally the story emerged.

Philip Barnes, Deputy Assistant of the Pacific Area desk of TASA had left the TASA building, over near the Reflecting Pool, bound for the Sears Building and the meeting about Karen Jenks.

Safford saw Rigsby knit his brows. Clearly the name Karen Jenks was teasing him. Oh well, it would come back, all too soon.

"Did you come over here with Barnes?" Rigsby asked.

"Eh? What?" Creighton had fallen into a brown study.

"The police," said Dr. Olivera with malice, "they are demanding our alibis!"

With some amusement, Safford observed that this undeniable fact created consternation. Señora Montoya was taken aback; Quentin Fels opened and shut his mouth. Zimmerman ran a beefy hand through rumpled hair.

"Oh, my God!" Creighton groaned. "Sorry, I've been thinking about TASA and how we'll get along without Phil. Then there's Ella Barnes . . ."

The police assured him that they would break the bad news to the Barnes home in Garrett Park. Creighton turned his attention to the question.

"No, Phil left some time before me. You can check with my secretary—oh, I'd say about ten or fifteen minutes. I had a last-minute call and I didn't want to hold things up."

Creighton himself had reached the Sears Building at about ten-fifteen. He had nodded to Dr. Olivera in the lobby, taken the elevator to the twelfth floor, detoured into the men's room where he encountered Carl Zimmerman, then proceeded to Room 1208. No, he had at no time seen Barnes.

"Uh-huh," said Rigsby while in the corner of the room a policeman took notes, "tell me about Barnes. What was he like?"

Creighton was nonplused. Safford would guess that he had never thought about his associate as a human being. "Phil? Well, he's a hard worker. Been with TASA—oh, about four or five years. He's really kept our shipment program running smoothly. Had an eagle eye for details. Pretty quiet fellow, otherwise." Howard Creighton came to a halt rather helplessly and cast around for more to add. "He's active in his church."

"Uh-huh," said Captain Rigsby again. If he wanted perceptive interpretation of Phil Barnes, he was going to have to look elsewhere for it. "Tell me, did you folks deal with Barnes?" He was addressing the Nuevadorians.

Señora Montoya plunged into thoughtfulness, then surprised Safford by saying: "No—o. No, I do not believe I met him. As cultural attaché . . ."

"I did," said Olivera without allowing her to finish. "We frequently reviewed the aid shipments to Nuevador. Mr. Barnes was correct." There was no warmth in this testimonial, but Dr. Olivera did not have Señora Montoya's expansive style with Americans.

"OK," said Rigsby. "Now, Dr. Olivera, can you tell me what you did this morning?"

"I came to the Sears Building," said Olivera. "I nodded to Mr. Creighton, then I recalled I had no matches. After I procured some, I came upstairs and waited."

"Right. You didn't come upstairs with Creighton or anybody you knew?"

"No."

"And did you come over from the Embassy with Señora Montoya here?"

"No."

Manuel Olivera was not going to explain. Was Rigsby struck, as Ben Safford was, with the disinclination of any of

32

these people to remain in the company of the others more than necessary?

"I did not come from the Embassy," Señora Montoya explained gently. "I was downtown, so I arrived directly here. I stopped downstairs to talk with Miss Engleman for a few moments. She is in charge of the Sears Fund medical training program in my country."

She made it sound as if it were not also Olivera's.

"Oh I must have missed you!" cried Quentin Fels unguardedly. Finding himself the focus of all eyes, he blushed and admitted that he had spent several minutes in the lobby, hoping to be able to welcome Señora Montoya. Since there were two entrances, he had missed her—and others.

This brought a sardonic smile to Manuel Olivera, but Señora Montoya remained unmoved.

"I see."

Carl Zimmerman, like Benton Safford, had left his office, driven to the Sears Building in time for the meeting and proceeded directly to Room 1208.

"Except for that trip to the men's room," Rigsby reminded him.

"Oh yes," said Zimmerman. "Yes, I forgot that."

"Anybody got anything else to add?" Rigsby asked.

Benton Safford, for one, did not. But somebody else did. It gave him, and others, food for thought.

"I do not know if it is of interest," said Señora Montoya with a sad half-smile. "As I was coming to this room, I did decide that it might be wise for me to speak to Mrs. Jenks. Sometimes only a woman can understand another woman . . ."

She was serenely sure of their attention. Manuel Olivera shot her a venomous look and even Quentin Fels was biting his lip.

"Mrs. Jenks," that rich voice went on imperturbably, "was not at her desk." She raised her eyebrows ruefully, despite

33

the glowering looks she was getting. "I thought perhaps you would want to know this."

Howard Creighton looked fully as thunderous as Ben Safford felt. For some reason, Señora Montoya was deliberately emphasizing Karen Jenks. Ben was unpleasantly reminded of a large, beautiful tigress.

Rigsby looked at her for a moment. "Nobody mentioned that this Karen Jenks is here in the Sears Building. She *is* the one who got thrown out of Nuevador, isn't she?"

Several voices rose, amplifying, correcting, supplementing.

Señora Montoya was now studying her magnificent diamond rings.

Finally Quentin Fels managed to compose a reply. "The Sears Foundation acceded to many—er—requests from a variety of sources to ask Mrs. Jenks to return from Nuevador. But she is and remains a Sears Scholar. And until her plans are clarified, Mrs. Jenks has a desk here in Washington."

As a statement, this left much to be desired, so Ben Safford was not surprised to hear criticism. It did not come, however, from the State Department, TASA or Nuevador, or even the Washington police. It came from behind him.

"Horseshit!"

Captain Rigsby proved equal to this. "You," he said turning around without excitement, "you must be Mrs. Jenks."

As Safford had feared, it was. Another premonition was also confirmed; Karen Kimball Jenks was a declared enemy of many aspects of modern society, but her deepest hostility was reserved, it soon developed, for the police.

"I am. And I'd like to know what right this thug of yours has to force me in here," she demanded, eyes blazing.

The thug was the uniformed policeman firmly grasping her arm. He had a long scratch on his cheek. He was about to reply when Rigsby nodded.

"OK, Flaherty. Oh, you'd better get that scratch attended to. I understand these things can turn nasty."

With a grin, Flaherty obeyed and, against a background

of discreet clucking, Safford relaxed. He was relieved. Karen Kimball Jenks could tie most of the adult world into knots, but Rigsby had just reminded Safford that the Washington D.C. Police Force had more experience than most with youth in revolt against authority.

"Sit down, Mrs. Jenks," said Captain Rigsby.

"Why should I?"

"Sit down, Karen," said Benton Safford firmly. He produced respect on several faces and, perhaps, a hint of amusement from Captain Rigsby.

Quentin Fels again spoke for the Sears Foundation. "Now, let's just wait a minute. I cannot permit . . ."

"Oh, for God's sake," said Karen Jenks wearily.

Firmly, Captain Rigsby silenced the outburst of comment and extracted an account of Karen Jenks' morning. She had spent most of her morning at her desk. Like everyone else being questioned, she had been on the premises but had no watertight alibi. She admitted several absences from her office.

"Yes," said Rigsby. "Señora Montoya says she stopped by when you weren't there."

Karen tossed the long mane of hair angrily.

"There's no law that I have to be glued to my desk! And I was getting ready for an open conference, not a lot of private deals! I have the right to—"

Oddly enough, it was Dr. Olivera who took exception to the suggestion of private deals. He rose to his colleague's defense.

"You talk too much about rights, Mrs. Jenks, and not enough about responsibilities."

"Oh I do, do I?"

Before Rigsby could reimpose order, everybody was shouting.

"Enough!" said Señora Montoya commandingly, with a very feminine look of dislike at Karen Jenks. Señora Montoya was a beautiful woman, beautifully turned out. But she

35

was not twenty-two. Ben wondered if personal jealousy explained her troublemaking. "I wish to cooperate with American authorities in every way, but this is enough! If you have any further questions, you may reach me at my Embassy! Now I shall go!"

She was on her imperious way when Captain Rigsby took the wind out of her sails. "I guess you can all go," he said. "We know where we can reach you. We're going to have to check out all these rooms here."

Karen Kimball Jenks obviously regarded this as anticlimax, if not betrayal. She had, as Ben Safford saw, unlimited willingness to take on all comers.

"Let's go, Mrs. Jenks," he said hastily. "You and I should have a little talk."

"Talk," she repeated with contempt. "What good is talk! I want some action."

Quentin Fels was eying her with an unfathomable expression. The other men, however, had hastily convened a conference and were deep in discussion. Captain Rigsby had turned to consult a subordinate.

"You might remember," said Safford sternly, "that somebody else wanted action today, and took it!"

He was pleased to see Karen Kimball Jenks look briefly shaken.

Chapter 4

Obviously the death of Philip Barnes of TASA was just the beginning. Murder alone could create plenty of embarrassment for any politician. God alone knew what a police investigation would do. And Ben Safford knew that the Washington police were not likely to be deflected by diplomatic immunity or political fallout.

But, as he sat at his desk the next afternoon, Safford did not realize there was further violence in store. That, however, was what Doug Travers seemed to expect when he called from the Sears Building.

"Karen's not here," Doug said tensely. "She's gone on the warpath!"

"So long as it's not my scalp she's after, I don't mind," said Ben bluntly. "Did she leave the reprints of that picture for you?"

Travers did not answer the question.

"You don't understand. She's gone haring off after Olivera."

"Olivera!" Ben exclaimed. "But she barely knows him."

37

"She's planning to start the acquaintance in a big way."
Travers sounded increasingly grim.

"But why Olivera?" Ben protested. "She was foaming at
the mouth about American authorities, the last I heard."

"You can thank Quentin Fels for this. He had a brain-
storm, and decided to call Karen Jenks in for a talk. He
decided"—and here Douglas Travers' voice rose in furious
parody—"to explain to her the undesirability of letting the
press learn the reason for that meeting yesterday morning.
And the misinterpretation that might be placed on her own
threats if she did not heed his warning."

Ben sighed deeply. If anybody asked, he would put Karen
Jenks' fighting weight at three times Quentin Fels'—easily.

"And so?" he asked.

"You can imagine what happened," Doug said bitterly.
"She fought back. And Fels got so rattled, he let the cat out
of the bag."

"What cat?" Ben asked quickly.

"It seems that TASA didn't recall Karen on its own hook.
There was an informal request from some Nuevadorians.
When she heard that, Karen ran up the flag. She claimed
that no American citizen had to sit still for that sort of thing
and said she was going to have Olivera's blood. So Fels
just let her go charging off to the Nuevadorian Embassy.
Where," he wound up furiously, "she's probably staging a
Bay of Pigs invasion all by herself!"

"Why Olivera? Was he the one who requested the recall?"
Ben asked.

"Hell, no! It was the Montoya crowd. They always try to
soft-pedal anti-American propaganda."

Ben didn't like the sound of things. Karen Jenks was in
enough trouble already. Stirring up a hornet's nest among
the Nuevadorians would do her cause no good.

"I'm going after her," he announced. "We've got to pull
her out of there."

"Shall I meet you there?" Doug offered.

But Ben decided, the fewer the better.

After a dramatic taxi ride, Safford alighted at the Nuevadorian Embassy. It was not one of Washington's modern architectural buildings, but an old mansion, protected by a high iron fence. When Safford mounted the steps and passed into the large reception area, he observed enough ornate gilt chairs, Oriental rugs, and gleaming chandeliers to know that the Nuevadorians were not economizing. There seemed to be a rule in South America: corrupt generals liked luxuries, but so did reform governments. If anybody went in for austerity, they were doing it at home.

He saw a young woman at a Louis XIV desk and several visitors waiting for officials. But there was no sign of Karen Jenks.

Of course, Ben reflected to himself, Mrs. Jenks was not designed by nature to wait.

Then he urged himself to think positively; there was no noise or excitement. No screams, thuds or yells of rage echoed down the graceful white stairwell. Assistants were not rushing to call the police, the FBI, the National Guard, or the little men with straitjackets.

"I am Mrs. Karen Jenks' Congressman," he said tentatively to the receptionist.

She was helpful. "Yes, sir. Mrs. Jenks is with Dr. Olivera now."

This was what Safford had hoped to avoid, but he said calmly: "Yes, they're expecting me to join them. I'm afraid I'm late."

Happily the receptionist was vivacious, petite, and far too concerned with her own image to question anything announced to her in a voice of authority.

"Certainly, Mr. Safford," she said, "I'll have a messenger take you right up."

So far, so good. There would be no calls upstairs to see if he was welcome, no time for Olivera to set the scene, no opportunity for a fresh display of belligerence by Karen

Jenks. Nothing but a soft-footed boy quietly padding up-stairs and down a richly carpeted hallway. Then there was a courteous knock, a door was opened for the announce-ment "Congressman Safford," and the boy was standing aside to show the surprised face of Nuevador's economic counselor.

But Dr. Olivera was not half so surprised as Benton Saf-ford. Unlikely as it seemed, Manuel Olivera and Karen Jenks were having a harmonious exchange about Nuevador and its problems. You could not call it placid. Probably no discussion with Karen Jenks ever was. Nor could you call it particularly sensible. Just now Karen was lecturing Olivera about his native land.

But she was not savagely blaming him for poverty in South America; she was not accusing him of corruption; she was not flatly claiming that he had thrown Philip Barnes out of a window to cover up his own delinquencies. More to the point, she was not berating him for her own predica-ment.

Safford advanced, smiling amiably, and said that he had been trying to track down Mrs. Jenks and hoped he wasn't intruding.

Dr. Olivera was courteously skeptical.

"Mrs. Jenks and I have been discussing the failure of American economic aid in Nuevador," he said. "Many of us have had doubts all along, of course. The aid is not in-tended by America to cure any of our ills, merely to stifle our own efforts at improvement, our own attempts to change the status quo."

The remark was meant to provoke a retort from Safford, but it never had a hope of getting past Olivera's other visitor.

"Thirteen crates," said Karen emphatically. "Each one as big as a room. I saw them with my own eyes, down at the docks. And do you know where that TASA aid was going to wind up? I'll tell you! In a week it would be in the hands of every corrupt little black marketeer in Nuevador. People would be starving in shantytown, while *they* were selling dried milk and eggs at a stinking fat profit!"

Manuel Olivera nodded agreement with a condescending smile. Safford knew the type, he decided. For some reason, a lot of embassies in Washington were staffed with one version or another of Dr. Olivera. He was intellectual; he was incorruptible; he was anti-American.

"Mrs. Jenks has seen the situation in my country and she is disturbed. Quite rightly so, in my opinion," he explained to Safford. "Naturally, her response is emotional. She sees injustice and she is outraged. It is what we all wish in our wives and daughters." He smiled at Karen with surprising warmth, then his voice hardened. "But educated men must look at these affairs differently. These are problems which must be solved with the brain, not the heart. The answer is not to throw a few illiterate black marketeers into prison. It is to attack the poverty at its roots, at its class orientation."

For once, Karen Jenks failed to live up to Safford's expectations. If he had dismissed her brain to approve her heart, she would probably have thrown the desk set at him. But here she sat, placidly listening to Olivera's comments without a single sign of mutiny.

"I haven't come to argue about American aid programs," he said good-naturedly. "I've been trying to get some reprints from Mrs. Jenks of that beach photograph of her. You understand, there is a question about its having been superimposed on that cathedral picture."

This was as close as Safford dared come to his real worry: had Karen accused Olivera of causing her recall? He got his answer just the same.

"There's no question at all about it," Karen intervened. "Anyone can see what happened. The two poses are absolutely identical. Just look at the way my hair is whipping

41

around. Is anyone claiming that there was a high gale in that cathedral?"

Olivera shrugged irritably. His hawk-eyed countenance became indifferent.

"Myself, I do not much care," he said frankly. "There has never been any concealment about my position. Nuevador can do without American aid, it can do without American students. They all come with strings attached. If you can prove that the photograph was falsified, go ahead. It will not do you much good. The damage has been done. I have already explained to Mrs. Jenks that I was not responsible for her recall." A sudden smile revealed white teeth. "Indeed, I would have preferred to have her remain and exacerbate the situation. My government would finally realize how much damage you Americans do."

One thing you had to say for Karen Jenks, Safford decided. She accepted a candor from other people that matched her own.

"I didn't go to Nuevador to do good," she said roundly. "I went there to do my own research. And this kangaroo court has balled everything up! I can't do my work anyplace else."

Manuel Olivera rose in Safford's opinion by saying that he couldn't care less about her research. Nuevador had enough problems of its own and, anyway, she was merely passing the time until she got married.

Karen Jenks inhaled deeply. "Married!" she spat. "I've been married and, in my opinion, you can give it back to the Indians!"

What Olivera would have replied they never found out. At that moment the door opened. Señora Luisa Montoya had decided to join them.

"I trust I am not disturbing you, Dr. Olivera," she said, as both men rose. "But there is a matter I would like to discuss with you."

"Not at all, Señora. You will remember that we met Mrs. Jenks and Congressman Safford yesterday."

Dr. Olivera was exceedingly polite. But his languor was gone. He was as intense as Safford remembered him yesterday at the Sears Building. If Karen Kimball Jenks interested him, Luisa Montoya triggered stronger emotions. As she came in and gracefully sank into a chair, Safford understood why Señora Montoya was an enigma. Magnificently indifferent to black looks from Karen Jenks, she was vibrantly self-possessed. With Olivera—the intellectual, the reformer, the man who believed in the new Nuevador of the common man rather than the old Nuevador of privilege and corruption—Señora Montoya was impeccably charming.

Yet Ben Safford was in no doubt about the emotion that pervaded the room. Manuel Olivera and Luisa Montoya hated each other.

Ben glanced at Karen Jenks, wondering if she, too, felt this. Perhaps so. She had stiffened.

"That unfortunate meeting yesterday," Señora Montoya's contralto proceeded. "What a tragedy! I hope Dr. Olivera has expressed our shocked concern—not only for your country, but for Mrs. Barnes—and her children."

Karen could not reply to this kind of woman. This left Ben to accept Nuevador's condolence.

Señora Montoya then turned to Karen directly. "And you will be going back to the Sears Foundation, I know. I hope you will transmit our regrets to Mr. Fels. Tell him that we will cooperate in any way we can, with regard to Mr. Barnes' death."

It was a shame, Ben thought, that these Nuevadorians were not more transparent. Just exactly what was going through Señora Montoya's mind?

Ben recalled her actions at the Sears Building, particularly her delicate, yet deliberate, insistence on pushing Karen Jenks into the center of a murder investigation.

At the time, he recalled, he had wondered if it might be

43

plain, old-fashioned, feminine jealousy. Now he knew he had been wrong.

Manuel Olivera would not hate—or fear—a woman whose behavior stemmed from anything so simple.

Still, Ben had to hand it to these Latins. The atmosphere was electric with emotions that he did not comprehend, but the niceties were being observed to a meticulous degree. In its way, it was admirable. It was also, Ben thought, rather terrifying.

Señora Montoya's last remark touched off a response from Olivera. Smoothly, he expanded the arena of her cooperation.

"I must explain to you, Señora, that you may be under a misapprehension. Mrs. Jenks has called to discuss her own problem. She wishes, quite understandably, to know the attitude of the Nuevadorian Government concerning a reexamination of her recall."

Olivera was mocking Señora Montoya. It was the Montoya forces, not Olivera, who had demanded Karen's recall. His dark eyes were openly amused. Señora Montoya, after all, was pro-American. She could not afford to emerge as Karen Jenks' persecutor.

And, in many ways, it was amusing. Olivera understood the situation. Señora Montoya understood. And so did Ben Safford.

This left Karen. Her blazing intensity left no room for what was not expressed in words. She might dislike Señora Montoya; she did not recognize an enemy.

Señora Montoya, however, could deal with threats. Without a flicker of hesitation, she gravely answered Olivera:

"Naturally, we Nuevadorians are concerned that there should be no miscarriage of justice. Mrs. Jenks' rights must be protected. It would be deplorable if it should develop that TASA acted with undue haste."

The lady was daring Olivera to reveal her secrets. Apparently it was not a challenge he cared to meet. Señora

44

Montoya left him in silence for a few moments, then shifted into formal leavetaking. As Olivera looked on with hooded eyes, she held out her hand to Karen.

"I am pleased you came to visit us. Rest assured, Mrs. Jenks, that my government will undertake a rigorous investigation of that disgraceful scene in our cathedral."

Karen started to reply, but Señora Montoya had turned to Ben Safford. He was ahead of her.

"You have been very helpful already," he said. "Mrs. Jenks and I are grateful."

He had the satisfaction of seeing a fleeting shadow of doubt in those velvet eyes.

After that, somehow, they were in the hall. Karen shook herself, and resentfully discovered that she had been cavalierly dismissed.

"But I haven't finished talking to Manuel—" she began.

Safford steered her firmly toward the staircase. "And do you think you could get anything out of him now?"

"Not with that man-eating tigress undulating around," she said.

Safford looked down at her. Karen, too, had noticed Señora Montoya's lithe and graceful walk. She was a woman who would ride, dance and ski superbly. Was Karen Jenks' spite the result of personal interest in Manuel Olivera? That would be a nice kettle of fish! Oh well, his immediate job was to get her out of the building. Ben continued down the stairs while she discontentedly cast glances over her shoulder. One of the troubles with this girl was that she never gave up. She was quite capable of bolting back to the office. Fortunately, as they rounded the curve, a figure at the reception desk provided a distraction.

"There's Carl Zimmerman," Ben said with deliberate provocation. "You've stirred up the State Department."

"Who? Oh, him." Unconsciously she responded. "I suppose all the little pansies at State go white at the thought of a plain American citizen in a foreign embassy."

Pansy was not the word Ben Safford would have used to describe Zimmerman's football-player hulk.

Carl Zimmerman had sighted them. He was obviously relieved to see Safford.

"Fels called me," he explained. "How much damage did she do?"

Karen started to ruffle up.

"Look," she exploded, "I've got a perfect right to—"

Unceremoniously Ben interrupted. He was beginning to learn some ground rules.

"None, I think," he said judiciously. "Olivera got her off onto the horrors of Nuevadorian poverty."

Zimmerman considered this, while Karen seethed.

"He's smooth," the man from State said finally. "And he knows what he's doing."

"Yes," Safford agreed, hoping that the frantic semaphoring of his eyebrows made it clear that now was not the time to introduce Señora Montoya's name.

In any event, Zimmerman, too, was beginning to adopt the brutal simplicity that seemed to work with Karen Jenks.

"Fels wants to see you," he said to her. "Why don't we put you into a taxi? I want a word with the congressman."

And, in spite of her reluctance, that was exactly what they did. As the two men stood watching the cab merge into the afternoon rush hour traffic, Safford turned to his companion.

"That's a good idea, Carl. I think it's about time we had a talk."

Chapter 5

Carl Zimmerman gave a massive sigh and indicated a Hot Shoppe across the street.

"All right," he said resignedly, "but we may as well be comfortable about it."

Once they were installed over their coffee, Zimmerman fell naturally into the only posture comfortable for two-hundred-pound men in small booths. Sitting kitty-corner with his back to the wall, he stretched out his legs diagonally, thrust his arm over the back of the booth, and opened the conversation with a question.

"How much do you know about Nuevador, Ben?"

"I don't know as much as you do," said Safford. "On the other hand, I've spent some time listening to testimony. And I do occasionally get to read a newspaper . . ."

Zimmerman chomped his way through a raised doughnut and frowned. He was dealing, Ben saw, with a common problem. Carl Zimmerman knew everything there was to know about Nuevador, from agriculture to zoology. How could he boil down this mass of expert knowledge into a few useful generalities?

Zimmerman laid down the doughnut. "Nuevador is in a very critical position at the moment. You remember General Vallon?"

"Sure," said Ben. "He was their dictator for years. He skipped, with blondes and money. He's been living in the South of France for the last year or two . . ."

Carl Zimmerman looked tempted to correct this. Instead, he pushed on:

"That's basically right. Vallon was popular with the crowds. But his real power came from the old landed aristocracy. They—and the army—supported him. He left them alone and they let him and his buddies strip the country. None of the organized political groups could stomach him. Vallon tended to shoot his opponents—communists, reformers, any critics at all."

"That simplifies politics," said Ben with a grin. "I've been tempted myself."

Zimmerman grinned too, and went on: "But the inevitable happened. Vallon ran the country virtually into bankruptcy, then he took off."

"Good riddance," said Ben. "And meanwhile, back in Nuevador . . . ?"

"Meanwhile, back in Nuevador, everybody was taken by surprise. Vallon was the only one who knew a crisis was coming, and naturally he wasn't telling anybody. So now there is a half-baked coalition government, with a grab bag of different political interests. They're trying to be a modern, honest, reform bunch—but they're weak. They don't have a lot of popular support yet, and they're pretty inexperienced. So, they're scared to death of the Vallonistas, who are still powerful throughout the country."

"Including the army, no doubt," said Ben. "Tell me about U.S. policy, Carl."

The man from the State Department grimaced. "You know the drill, Ben. We recognized the old Vallon regime—so people are claiming that we're in favor of dictatorship.

48

And this new bunch is trying to cash in on this and whip up some popular enthusiasm with a little well-placed propaganda about Yankee imperialism, and Nuevador for Nuevadorians. We're being very, very careful."

Ben thought for a moment. "How much good will being careful do if Olivera's typical of this new bunch?"

Carl Zimmerman did not know.

There was a moment of bemused silence while the Hot Shoppe bustle eddied around the booth. Then Zimmerman summarized: "So, the country is trembling on the brink of a revolution—and Vallon and his gang are waiting in the wings."

"Waiting for everyone to remember the good old days, eh? That's a familiar trick," Ben said.

"Every day that passes makes his position stronger. That's the real time pressure on the situation. Nuevador is ripe for an explosion in one direction or another."

Safford groaned. "And into this setup marches Karen Kimball Jenks."

"Who claims the pictures of her that got published round the world were doctored." Zimmerman paused. "I never did get to see those snapshots yesterday."

"I'll have the enlargements circulated, but that's just a formality. I don't think there's any doubt about it. The snaps taken at the ocean show her in a perfectly natural pose, jumping for a beach ball. Somebody just superimposed them on the cathedral pictures."

"A put-up job," Zimmerman said softly.

"Yes. I'm sure the experts will bear this out."

"I didn't mean just the pictures."

The two men eyed each other hesitantly. Ben had known this was coming. He decided to take the bull by the horns.

"I've been thinking about that, too. The whole business of a girl in a bikini gate-crashing church services and acting like a maniac is too crazy to be genuine. This isn't simply a case of somebody capitalizing on an incident by falsifying a

49

picture. First, they got the snapshot of Karen Jenks. Then, they deliberately staged an incident into which they could incorporate it. The whole thing started with somebody spotting Karen as the ideal subject for anti-American propaganda."

"Spotting her—or importing her."

Safford was taken aback. Carl Zimmerman was not fighting him. On the contrary, he was racing ahead with further speculation:

"Look, Ben, there are approximately fifteen American graduate students in Nuevador. I don't count the scientists. They're all five hundred miles upriver with no one around but alligators and mosquitoes. Nuevador isn't a big country and it doesn't draw a lot of foreign students. The few that do come tend to be pretty serious-minded. Normally, you could wait twenty years before a Karen Jenks showed up in Nuevador. Maybe somebody struck it lucky. But I'm beginning to think it's too lucky to be coincidental."

Safford grappled with the implications of this speech. At the very least, it meant complicity by the Sears Foundation. And, if they handled their appointments the way they handled their recalls, it could mean complicity by TASA, the State Department, or even the Nuevadorian Embassy. Why couldn't the damned girl have been somebody else's constituent?

"You've left out one thing, Carl," he finally said.

"I have?"

"Yes," said Ben gently. "As soon as a serious investigation of the cathedral incident was proposed, Philip Barnes, who was an official from TASA, seems to have gotten himself murdered!"

Zimmerman's eyes widened. He was too experienced to blurt out his first thoughts. Only after a minute did he speak.

"I never even thought of that," he said.

"I'll bet the police did," said Ben.

He was right.

Carl Zimmerman may not have been thinking about the murder of Philip Barnes. The Sears Foundation was forced to.

The police had not only sealed off the twelfth floor of the Sears Building, they were active elsewhere. Quentin Fels was already a badly rattled man when Captain Rigsby reappeared for another round of questioning.

"I see no need for all this," Fels protested, referring to the phalanx of police specialists fanning throughout the building, asking questions, disrupting work, photographing, measuring.

Captain Rigsby was unmoved.

"Maybe you don't," he said. "But yesterday, somebody cracked Philip Barnes over the head with that bookend and pushed him out of a window. That's murder, Mr. Fels. I don't know how the Sears Foundation looks at it, but the police take it pretty seriously."

Fels tried to speak; Rigsby pushed on. "I want some background on this Jenks girl—and her trip down to Nuevador."

Fels was sputtering: "But that has nothing to do with this—accident."

"No accident, Mr. Fels," Rigsby contradicted sharply. "And since Phil Barnes was important in these TASA shipments to Nuevador, and you folks were having a conference about Karen Jenks and Nuevador—well, it looks to us as if maybe Nuevador enters into things."

"I disagree—"

But Rigsby was implacable. Finally, he forced Quentin Fels to review the entire Nuevadorian program of the Sears Foundation.

The Sears Foundation, Fels said, soothed by the act of talking, supported hundreds of scholars each year. The basic goal of the Foundation was to make possible research which might otherwise never be undertaken. "Real scholarly research," said Fels, "is often a time-consuming business. We're not interested in run-of-the-mill projects. Why, most of our scholars already have their Ph.D.s. Most of our research is very advanced—"

Rigsby held up a hand. "OK. Stop right there. Why did you pick up this Jenks girl? She's just a kid. She's not one of your high-powered scholars—so far as I can see. Did you have any special reason—say, like a recommendation from Barnes?"

"No!"

Rigsby was watching Fels closely. "Did Mrs. Jenks have any special connections with Nuevador?"

"No!" screeched Fels. "At least, not that I know of!"

Rigsby continued to ask questions that Fels could not answer, finally driving him into a frenzy.

"Look, Captain," he said with a voice that trembled. "I was speaking about most of the work that the Sears Foundation sponsors. We do reserve some grants for graduate students. And Mrs. Jenks got one of them. That's all there was to it. Her qualifications and her field of research were reviewed by our usual board. They were quite satisfied." He looked at Rigsby to see if he was making an impression. "It was pure routine, I assure you. Just now, of course, I am planning to revise our procedures, so that we put more emphasis on the personality of our people. But as for Mrs. Jenks and Nuevador—well, she was interested in Nuevador. And as for why she was—well, you'll have to ask her!"

He halted abruptly, as if hearing his own words for the first time. Rigsby however was stolid.

"I was intending to, Mr. Fels. Don't you worry about that. I was intending to."

Karen Jenks was seated in the small cell that was her office. She was not doing any research. She was talking impassionedly to a young man dressed in tight jeans and an army surplus jacket. When Captain Rigsby, massive and uniformed, appeared in the doorway, two pairs of eyes looked at him with automatic hostility.

"You with the Sears Foundation, too?" Rigsby asked the young man.

"No." It was a masterpiece of insolence.

But perhaps there was another reaction as well, for the young man got to his feet. "Guess I'll be getting on, Karen," he said, twisting his lips into a knowing smile. "See you tonight."

He was planning to ignore the policeman. The whole effect was spoiled when Rigsby did not budge in the doorway. For a moment, they confronted each other. Then, deliberately, Rigsby moved forward. The young man took a step backward, then hurriedly exited.

"Who was that?" Rigsby asked.

"A friend of mine," said Karen Jenks with an angry flush.

"What's his name?"

Rigsby might have been asking idle friendly questions, but he was not.

"Gallagher," said Karen Jenks, more angrily. "Russ Gallagher. What are you doing, checking up on all my—?"

Rigsby made a note of the name, then baldly told Mrs. Jenks to explain what had taken her to Nuevador. The rapid change of subject made her uneasy.

"I didn't pick Nuevador," she said, startled. "It picked me."

Rigsby waited. She looked impatient, but went on. "I wanted to do research in a smaller South American country, but I needed a fellowship from one of these foundations. Well, you've got to use your head. I heard that the Sears Foundation had become interested in Nuevador—so I said I wanted to study in Nuevador. It was as simple as that."

Rigsby weighed her reply. It might be as simple as that. It was not the way Quentin Fels had put it. Making another note to look further into Sears' activities in Nuevador, he asked:

"Did you know Philip Barnes?"

Resentment, and anxiety, again flared. "No," she said firmly. "That is, I met him when I got back here. He was a sanctimonious hypocrite, if you want to know! He said that he would pray for guidance about my problems!"

She gave a short, contemptuous laugh.

Mildly, Captain Rigsby said, "That doesn't seem too bad. Not bad enough to get a man murdered."

Karen Jenks stared blindly at him. "No," she finally whispered. "I guess it isn't."

Chapter 6

By Sunday night Benton Safford was beginning to feel that, for a congressman who had been at the scene of a murder, he was going to be very, very lucky. The Washington Police Force, unlike almost every other official body in the capital, seemed to prefer action to words. Ben's week end had been punctuated by a dozen phone calls from acquaintances; some were kindly, some curious, some warning. But they all delivered the same basic message. The police were asking if Congressman Safford had ever had anything to do with Philip Barnes, with TASA, with Nuevador. Ben already knew that Madge, Doug Travers, the guard at the door of the House Office Building, and the taxi dispatcher immediately outside had each been queried about his departure for the Sears Building on the morning of Philip Barnes' death. But, in spite of this far-flung underground activity, Captain Rigsby was being unusually discreet in his press releases. According to these statements, the police were not satisfied that Mr. Barnes' fall had been an accident. The city's newspapers had been left with the impression that there was a possibility of suicide and, wary of

55

being sued by the dead man's family, had given the story minimal coverage.

This discretion had won gratitude in more than one quarter. The Nuevadorian Embassy, thankful to be spared the disgrace of two diplomats involved in scandal, was overlooking minor irritants such as Karen Jenks' intrusion into their premises. Señora Montoya, herself, had calmed Quentin Fels' fears on the subject. The Sears Foundation and TASA were just as relieved as Safford. Everyone, it seemed, had been dreading front-page notoriety.

But Monday had not run its course for long before Ben was reminded that he had forgotten somebody who had absolutely no use for a reticent maintenance of the status quo. The phone call from Howard Creighton at TASA came through just as he was preparing to leave for the House floor.

"I'm sorry to bother you, Congressman, but things are getting out of hand."

Creighton's gravel voice was not excited, but it was packed with urgency.

"Have the police got a line on Barnes' murder?" Safford asked, surprised.

"The police?" Creighton repeated vaguely. "I don't think so. They've got a couple of detectives nosing around here. And they've been driving his wife crazy. But the papers would have picked it up if they had a lead."

"I thought we were all getting a break on the publicity," Ben said frankly.

"We were." Creighton was grim. "But it's not Phil's murder I'm calling about. A friend of mine at UPI tipped me off to look at the early afternoon editions."

The familiar premonition gripped Safford. Again it was justified. Karen Jenks had lost patience with official tactics. After consulting Russ Gallagher, she had decided to take her case to the people. The evening papers in Washington, and elsewhere, were carrying a long interview with her.

56

In it, she provided a very graphic description of her treatment in Nuevador and accused the Sears Foundation and TASA of trampling her rights as an American citizen. Furthermore she had, at last, turned her attention to the motive for her frame-up. She had been expelled, she decided, because corruption in Nuevador could not survive scrutiny by a clear-eyed intelligence. The words *fascist, militarist,* and *establishment* figured heavily in her remarks.

"But that's not the worst," Creighton summarized angrily. "She's given out those damned beach pictures. In Washington, anyway, they're heading the story with two pictures —the cathedral one and the beach ball one. Right on the front page. Jesus Christ, you'd think she'd learn to avoid bikini poses!"

Ben Safford understood Creighton's response but not his reasons for calling. He said so.

"Look," said Creighton, "I was just wondering if you can't do something about that kid!"

"I take that as a compliment," said Safford, "but I don't see what I can do. Mrs. Jenks—as you know—is a handful."

There was a rumble of agreement. When Creighton again spoke, he was more a man relieving himself of troubles than a seeker of aid.

"Sure, sure," he growled. "God, what a mess! And all this publicity is the last thing we need. Nobody ever realized just how much Phil Barnes was on top of all the shipment details for Nuevador. Hell, we had a dozen containers due for shipment to Montecigalpa last week—and they're still sitting in our warehouse over in Maryland. And once you get off schedule, you just fall farther and farther behind. Then you get them all on your neck—the Embassy, the State Department, Congress . . ."

"Yes," said Congressman Benton Safford dryly, but Creighton was too far gone to register irony.

"You know, Mr. Congressman, I don't want our whole

57

South American program to bog down. Especially in an election year."

Congressmen were not the only people in Washington to keep eyes cocked on forthcoming events.

"TASA has bipartisan support," Safford pointed out.

Howard Creighton knew Washington realities.

"TASA has bipartisan support as long as it works," he said bitterly. "Just let things start getting fouled up and the long knives will be out." He sank into gloomy silence, then abruptly said, "Well, Mr. Congressman, I'll personally appreciate anything you can do." Then he rang off.

This conversation gave Safford food for thought. Not that Howard Creighton had said anything startling. No, it was the fact of the call itself. Senior officials in large government agencies in Washington are not in the habit of calling congressmen to reveal bureaucratic breakdowns. Shipments falling behind schedule were no real index. It was Howard Creighton's call that told Ben how serious the trouble at TASA was. These thoughts accompanied him out of his office and toward Committee Room 1706 and the Ways and Means Subcommittee.

Two hours later, Ben Safford was ambling back with an entertaining interlude behind him. Since the subject at issue had been an appropriation for the Army Corps of Engineers, there had been the usual confrontation between the military and the civilian. The outcome might have been a toss-up, had it not been for the presence of Congresswoman Hollenbach (R., Cal.).

Elsie Hollenbach, a vigorous gray-haired leader of the League of Women Voters, the Consumers League, and many other organizations, was possibly the only member of either house of Congress who could fearlessly take on General Bartle and the whole Corps. As a result, her heavily suburban district just outside San Francisco had more dams and drainage control areas than it knew what to do with. Since Mrs. Hollenbach frequently voted against the Corps on appropriations, her colleagues were variously infuriated or bemused. Only a small minority of them realized that her success was due to an eye for essentials.

She had displayed that eye when walking back to the office block with Ben.

"You've been fortunate in your press coverage, Ben. I mean about that death at the Sears Building."

Ben agreed. He saw no reason to tell her what she would be reading in her evening paper.

"But I doubt if it can go on," Mrs. Hollenbach continued. "I know I'm not alone in thinking that an investigation of TASA may be required. So far there has been no hint of scandal, or graft. But when important economic officers jump out of windows—well, I, for one, don't like the implications!"

Re-entering his office, Ben found himself inclined to agree. Even without the Karen Jenks publicity, there was a small part of Washington that was chronically suspicious of mysterious death among high government officials.

"Oh, here he is now," Madge told the phone. She handed the receiver to Ben, saying: "Mr. Zimmerman, State."

Ben put it to his ear to hear Zimmerman already in full flight.

". . . my God, Ben, can't you do anything about that girl!"

This breakdown in Carl Zimmerman's normal imperturbability was easily explained; newspapers in Nuevador, Argentina, Mexico and Brazil had picked up the Karen Kimball Jenks' interview and were giving it heavy play.

"On a selective basis, of course," Carl snarled. "The Nuevadorians and the Cubans are just publishing the cathedral picture, together with one taken here in Washington where she's surrounded by a bunch of hippies. Fidel is going to make a speech about Yanqui degenerate imperialism. I've got the Secretary on my neck—and he's got the White House on his!"

Ben was strongly tempted to point out that, if the Jenks affair had not been mishandled from the start, all this high-level anguish could have been avoided, but the tide of complaint gave him no opening. Madge, listening unabashedly on her extension, was convulsed with silent mirth.

"Now look, Carl," Ben finally managed to edge into the conversation, "I don't like this any better than you do. Probably a lot less. But it's no worse than the publicity you were getting a month ago when all this broke. So why go ape?"

Zimmerman exercised control. His next words were delivered with unnatural calm.

"It *is* worse now. That's the point, Ben. The government of Nuevador is being put in an embarrassing position. Their press may only carry the cathedral picture, but there are plenty of Latin American papers that are going to have a field day with this. Hell, they're always on the lookout for sexy pictures anyway."

Safford said that the Washington papers were only human, too.

"Yes, yes." Zimmerman swept the interjection aside. "That's not important. We were hoping to keep this Jenks business the sort of dirty linen you wash in private. That's why the Embassy has been cooperating with us. Now, there's bound to be a first-class Nuevadorian mess."

"You'll have to explain that, Carl."

"So long as the villain of the piece was an American, the Nuevadorians could be united. And God knows they need to be! But as soon as the word leaks out that it was the Montoya crowd behind Karen Jenks' recall, they're going to be sitting ducks for an attack by the reformers."

"You mean because they made fools of themselves?" Ben asked. As a practicing politician, he could have told the diplomats that every party in every country in the world does that.

If Zimmerman's analysis was having little effect on Ben,

it was at least acting as a safety valve. Carl had grown a lot cooler.

"Sure. The Montoyas—you know the husband is in the cabinet back home—pose as pro-Americans. When an enormous anti-American scandal blows up, they try to hush it up or tamp it down as fast as possible. So they wind up falling for a fake that's so obvious anybody can see through it by just looking at two pictures."

The silence that greeted these remarks was so lengthy that Zimmerman's next words were: "Ben? Ben, are you still there?"

"I'm here all right, Carl." Safford had finally become a wholehearted participant in the exchange. "Do you realize you've just pinpointed the first solid motive for this frame-up? Suppose the reformers were in back of it, not for its anti-American value, but to undercut the Montoya crowd?"

This was not the kind of solace that the State Department was searching for. "Ben," Carl said firmly, "I won't deny that you've made a point. But could we just concentrate on the things we can do something about? Like gagging that Jenks girl?"

"I don't know what makes you put Karen on the list of things I can do something about." Ben rushed on to forestall argument. "But, all right. All right, I'll take steps."

He hung up before Zimmerman could ask what steps.

Both Madge and Doug Travers were now regarding Safford with interest. Doug was sharing the secretarial extension.

"Well, what else could I say?" Ben demanded.

Madge appeared to have a bag of playful suggestions, but Travers was more immediately helpful, although not in the way he intended.

"I think you're absolutely right, sir," he said. "We do have some sort of responsibility for this wild woman. It's obvious she's not capable of figuring anything out for herself."

Inspiration came.

"Doug," said Safford solemnly, "I'm going to have to ask you to track Karen down. I want you to try to talk some sense to her . . . er . . . away from the official atmosphere, if you see what I mean."

Doug saw all too clearly. His jaw clenched and he seemed on the verge of mutiny. But it was Madge who spoke.

"Now that, Mr. Safford, really is disgraceful of you!"

Chapter 7

Douglas Travers disliked the prospect of a turbulent interview with Karen Jenks. He knew it would be a failure, and he disliked failing. Usually he didn't, because he was ambitious, level-headed, and aggressive. He was shrewd enough to guess that these qualities might be more useful in a battle royal with Mrs. Jenks than in any attempt to talk sense to her. He decided to postpone her until the dinner hour. This left him free to tackle the FBI where he had no intention of failing.

The problem was Mrs. Raymond Huggins. Mrs. Huggins was the widow of a Special Agent who had been shot down by a crazed kidnapper. In the eyes of the FBI, Raymond Huggins had left a widow and three children. And, with the best will in the world, FBI administrative procedures could not seem to readjust to the birth of twins six months after Agent Huggins' death. The Huggins family was struggling to get by on a modest pension; Mrs. Huggins needed every penny she could get.

This sort of snarl could go on for months. But every day was a hardship for the Huggins family. Mrs. Huggins had been almost apologetic when she applied to her congressman for assistance. Doug Travers was determined that she was going to get it—and fast.

This was the kind of help that Ben Safford valued, and it was provided by only the best administrative assistants.

"Thank God for Travers!" Safford had told Madge not long after Doug was hired. "He's willing to take some of the real work off my shoulders. He doesn't want to sit around, writing policy speeches all the time."

Even Madge, who was not a consistent optimist about new staff, had been hopeful.

"He seems to be able to get things done—and, what's more, without rubbing people the wrong way."

Doug knew all about these assessments and continued to get things done. By five o'clock he was back at his own desk, phoning Newburg to inform the grateful Mrs. Huggins that the right check was already on its way. Then, as he typed out a report for Congressman Safford, Doug grinned briefly to himself: he could only hope that his meeting with Karen Jenks worked out as well as his meeting with the FBI. Arming himself with her address from the files, he left the office and set off on foot.

His first sight of 112 C Street did not surprise him. Unlike Benton Safford, Doug Travers had been at a large university less than a year ago. He knew all about communal living in large, dilapidated frame houses. There would be couples with children and without children, there would be couples mixed racially and couples unmixed sexually, there would be Zen Buddhists, political activists, and apprentice gurus. Somewhere there would also be Karen Jenks. The problem was to find her.

The front door stood open, so he advanced into the hallway and took inventory. On the hall table stood two large rucksacks, a kiddie carrier, a pile of books and a transistor radio. In the large room on the right front, six adults and two high chairs were gathered around a large table bearing wicker bottles of chianti and plates of pizza. On the left front, a folk group seemed to be in practice session. Two dejected-looking guitarists dandled their instruments and a girl vocalist slumped cross-legged on a floor cushion while a thin, intense man, who had swiveled away from the piano, glared at them savagely and said on a rising note: "No! No! No!"

Hastily Doug pushed on. There were smaller rooms to the rear. On the right, two bearded men stood amid a welter of photographic equipment. Surrounded by movie cameras, spotlights, large cans of film and yards of cable, they argued heatedly.

". . . and I say, unless you have created simultaneously an intellectual happening and a physical happening, all you get is an artistic void!"

"No!" said the red-haired one. "The audience has to provide its own intellectual content. By pushing out to the boundaries of sensation, you create a matrix . . ."

In the cubbyhole on the left, there was a sofa and a young couple making love passionately. Nowhere was there the slightest sign of Karen Jenks, or of any means to locate her. Doug briefly reviewed the possibilities and made a choice.

"Sorry!" he accosted the film-makers. "I'm looking for Karen Jenks. Do you know where she is?"

The two beards stopped waggling and faced him. Their owners examined Doug Travers' seeksucker suit and knotted tie. They did not like what they saw.

"Never heard of her," said the redhead briefly.

Doug knew better than to be friendlier than they were.

"Jenks," he repeated. "She lives here."

Redhead shrugged. "Not by me."

Doug Travers was suddenly glad that he was here, instead of Congressman Safford. He had gone to school with these people. In a situation that would certainly puzzle anyone over thirty, he knew exactly what to do. He had already spotted the stairs at the end of the hall. He marched directly to the center of the stairwell extending to the third floor, threw his head back, and with lungs developed by military training, bellowed:

"Jenks! Karen Jenks!"

Before the echoes died away, he was rewarded. A succession of faces, more inquiring than startled, popped over the railing. First, there was a rabbity-looking youth dripping in a bathrobe. Helpfully he too turned upward and piped:

"Karen! It's for you, Karen!"

Then there was a girl in a bath towel, oiled and flushed from the sunlamp. She pointed upward and said crisply:

"Third floor."

Finally from the very top, an unseen voice wafted downward.

"She's out."

Doug planted himself more firmly.

"When will she be back?"

This, in turn, produced a chorus of yodeling. Newcomers joined the relay. The old-timers drifted back to tubs and sunlamps. The entire uproar was dominated by the name "Maureen." And he had what he wanted. Maureen was the girl with information. Yelling at her to wait, he started to climb the stairs. She in turn started to descend. They met halfway.

Maureen's only notable feature was a cloud of black hair which she had been brushing. Throughout their conversation the rhythmic stroking continued.

Doug did not waste time with explanations. He simply stated his needs.

"I've got to find Karen Jenks. Do you know where she is?"

Maureen had no idea, but she volunteered the fact that Karen had been dressed up.

"Do you know when she'll be back?"

"No. But why don't you come back around eleven? They don't usually stay out late."

66

"They?" Doug asked.

"She went out with Russ Gallagher."

"Who is this Gallagher?"

"Oh, Russ lives here too."

"I meant, what does he do?"

Maureen, incurious until now, examined Doug with interest. But she replied readily: "He's a power in SDS over at George Washington University. You know the kind of thing—he's always occupying buildings and burning files."

This wasn't the kind of company Karen Jenks needed right now, Doug thought.

Maureen watched him in amusement. Her eyes were mischievous when she spoke.

"Karen's a fool."

Doug was in no position to argue but he had a hunch that he and Maureen were on different wave lengths.

"What do you mean?" he asked, in effect inviting her to put up or shut up.

Deliberately Maureen shifted the attack on her hair. Reversing the brush so that its bristles were upward, she slipped it under her mane and let loose a series of long, crackling strokes. She timed her speech to synchronize with her movements.

"Russ is only looking for a situation he can exploit. He doesn't give a damn about Karen. He just wants to move onto a bigger stage than George Washington."

Doug spoke more harshly than he intended. "She's a big girl. She can look after herself."

"Well, she hasn't done an outstanding job so far, has she?" Maureen said tartly.

This question followed Doug to a steak and beer at a tavern near Dupont Circle. He had cut off Maureen with a curt request for her to leave Karen a message. For some reason, confidences about Karen's romantic problems grated. But now, mellowed by food and drink, he found himself thinking about what she had said. There was something in it. Karen might be pretty damned infuriating. But she had been pretty damned unfortunate, too. First there was a marriage that didn't take, leaving her with a small child. Then, when she picked herself up and tried to make a new life for herself, she landed in the middle of a South American plot. It wasn't easy for Douglas Travers to think of Karen Jenks as a victim. But he had seen those photographs and he agreed with Ben Safford: Karen had been framed.

This amounted to a lot of bad luck for a beginner, Doug admitted. He might have gone further along these lines, but he was interrupted. Karen Jenks was speaking.

"They'll try to cover up everything they can get away with!" she said with ringing fervor.

"Precisely what do you accuse the authorities of covering up, Mrs. Jenks?" asked an unknown voice theatrically.

Doug looked around wildly, almost expecting to find Karen at the next table. But the people at the next table, like everyone else in the room, were silently looking at the wall. Doug followed their gaze—to a large, ceiling-hung television set. The seven o'clock panel program—*Washington Today*—was unfolding.

"They've covered up the way I was framed in Nuevador! Now the police are covering up the murder of Philip Barnes at TASA!"

"And do you think the two are connected, Mrs. Jenks?" prompted a panel member.

"I certainly do! I think I have a right to demand a full investigation into TASA's work in Nuevador," Karen proclaimed.

"Now, Mrs. Jenks, we know that you spent considerable time in Nuevador. What, in your opinion, was the effect of American aid to that country?"

Douglas Travers did not wait. He was already signaling for his check. He would go over to the studio and shut

68

her up for good, he promised himself. He would go over there and wring her neck, he thought, as he flung money at the cashier.

In the taxi, however, he did a little hard thinking. This had to be deliberate. All the discretion about Philip Barnes' murder had just been blasted sky high. Even worse, the murder was now publicly linked to TASA and Nuevador. This was the worst thing Karen Jenks had done yet. And she was old enough to know it.

Doug could see the shape of things to come: cries for Congressional action, investigators descending on TASA, and God-knew-what coming out of Nuevador. And, like too many innocent bystanders, Congressman Safford was sure to be swept into the fracas.

This spelled the end to any hope for a quick solution of Karen Jenks' problem. After this outburst, piecemeal concessions were doomed. Everybody concerned was going to stall until the big picture emerged. Well, Karen Jenks might be a victim, Doug thought grimly, but she was no longer looking for justice. Now she was out for blood.

The taxi had reached the TV studio. Doug was past the revolving door before he stopped dead. What was he doing here? He checked his watch. *Washington Today* still had another fifteen minutes to run. They weren't going to let him charge in and pull her off camera. But the Information Desk had a surprise for him. He was led immediately to a small reception room. There, cool and unruffled, sat Karen Jenks. With her was Russ Gallagher, very pleased with himself.

"What do you think of it?" she asked, waving to the set in the corner, from which her own image stared back at her.

Doug looked from her to the screen.

"I thought you were doing it live," he said.

"Oh, no, we taped at four-thirty this afternoon. They wanted their legal people to monitor it."

"You mean to say the lawyers let this through?"

"They cut a couple of sentences," said Karen indifferently.

"They must be crazy. The police department hasn't even announced that Barnes was murdered."

Russ Gallagher was triumphant. "They have now," he announced. "When the studio put the pressure on them, the cops confirmed a lot."

Doug was silent. Goaded, Gallagher continued:

"You thought you had everything all sewed up, didn't you? Well let me tell you, we just cracked it wide open!"

Doug had learned a long time ago to lose his temper when it was convenient for him, not for a Russ Gallagher.

"I'm surprised the TV people went along with you," he said smoothly.

Gallagher laughed shortly. "Listen, I've got a lot of contacts in the right places. It was a cinch to sell Karen. She's a natural for TV. I said: *Tell it like it is*—and that's what she did, didn't she? You wait until tomorrow. The big boys won't know what's hit them!"

Doug's expression did not alter, although two points were registering. Russ Gallagher was absolutely right. And so, by God, was Maureen! Karen Jenks was being exploited by this little bastard with an eye for the main chance. Russ Gallagher had set up the press conference yesterday, Russ Gallagher had lined up the TV cameras. Whether she knew it or not, Karen Jenks had become a puppet.

Doug decided to find out just how strong the strings were.

"Congratulations!" he said to her sardonically. "You've smeared TASA. You've accused a lot of people of murder. And you've knifed Ben Safford. Boy, you sure pick a funny way to get your kicks!"

"What do you mean, kicks?" Karen flared. "Have you forgotten that I've got a stake in this, too? I notice you've got a bleeding heart for every civil service nit! How come I don't rate any sympathy? Or do I have to fill out a form in triplicate to qualify?"

"You'd rate a hell of a lot more sympathy," he said deliberately, "if you used your head for a change."

"All I've rated so far is double talk. Now, I'm playing with a new set of rules. And, if you don't like them, you'd better sell your TV set—because you're going to be seeing a lot of me. And you're not going to like what I've got to say!"

Russ Gallagher lit a cigarette and leaned back, following the exchange appreciatively. "Forget about baby boy, here, Karen. Plenty of people will get the message. TASA is just the start. We're going on to bigger things."

Doug shot a look at Karen. That last sentence, he thought, might have backfired.

"I'm not interested in TASA being just a start!" she snapped. "And I'm not interested in going on to bigger things. What I want is to make them eat that recall. In public, under floodlights!"

Doug had what he wanted. Those strings were not so strong. It was going to be possible to drive a wedge between Karen Jenks and this half-baked Svengali. Not now, he knew, but in time. Now, there was very little he could do. With nothing to lose, he could afford to be honest.

"You've got delusions of grandeur, Karen," he said. "All you've proved is that you were the last person on earth to be sent to Nuevador, frame-up or no!"

"Great!" said Karen, rising. "Anybody who doesn't fall on their knees has got to be suppressed. Well, you're behind the times, buster. Suppressing's just gone out of style!"

She swept up her belongings.

"I'd watch where I was going, if I were you," Doug remarked.

Karen was already at the door, impatiently waiting for Gallagher.

"Don't you worry! I'm a big girl now. I can look after myself."

She was echoing his own words, Doug realized. By now, he was convinced they were wrong.

Chapter 8

On Monday, Karen Jenks appeared before a local TV audience on *Washington Today*. On Tuesday, she was a guest on the coast-to-coast *Today* show. By Wednesday, the dam had burst. There were, in rapid succession, a long personality sketch in *The New York Times*, a two-page feature in *Look* magazine, editorials in the *Christian Science Monitor*, headlines from Peking to Palo Alto and an avalanche of letters to the editor.

"And every damn one of them," Doug Travers said, indicating a pile of clippings, "pushes the same line. She's screaming corruption in Nuevador, corruption at TASA and a police cover-up of the Phil Barnes murder."

Safford was glancing over an item from *The Washington Post*. "She's doing some branching out. Here are some pretty harsh opinions about the average congressman, including me. Except that Mrs. Jenks seems to think I may be below average."

They were sitting in Ben's office. They should have been talking about Amendment II of the Agriculture Bill. Instead they were discussing Karen Jenks. It had been that kind of a week. Ben sighed.

Doug Travers was scowling. "You know," he said, "I still think, if we could get her away from Gallagher, we might make some progress."

Ben looked at his administrative assistant with weary amusement. "You're not still trying to convince me that Karen is an innocent tool of student activists, are you, Doug? You can't sell me."

Travers grinned in acknowledgment. "Not completely. I admit Karen is out to raise hell on her own. But she has a specific target. We might be able to do something about that. If Gallagher has any goal, it's a social revolution." He broke off with a shrug.

Ben detected sympathy for Karen Jenks. What's more, he understood it. The initial official response to her problems had been both insensitive and bungling. Now she was running her head against a stone wall. Ben did not much like the spectacle himself. No wonder someone twenty years younger did not either.

Spokesmen for TASA, the U. S. Department of State, and the government of Nuevador had announced that Mrs. Jenks' grievances stemmed from her recall from Montecigalpa. This matter was being taken under advisement. None of the responsible authorities were inclined to place credence in unfounded accusations and allegations. End of statement.

The Washington Police Department said that the death of Philip Barnes was being investigated. It was not Department policy to issue releases on pending cases. After that, official silence.

"It's not a bad tactic," Ben said reflectively. "If you go on in politics, Doug, you'll find that nothing makes anybody sound more hysterical and irresponsible than a dignified silence. They're trying to cut the ground out from under her."

73

"Yeah," said Travers. He did not sound enthusiastic. For that matter, Ben was not convinced that the official line could hold for long.

In the first place, press, radio and television seemed to find Karen Jenks—and even Russ Gallagher—irresistible. As a practicing politician, Ben knew better than to underestimate ratings. Then, in the second place, the public silence was covering a lot of in-fighting. The government of Nuevador was charging U.S. interference in its internal affairs. Federal authorities were nagging at the Washington Police Department. Ben himself had been getting more telephone calls than he cared to think about.

"And the trouble is," said Madge, when she came in to remind Safford of a committee meeting, "just about the time that the story shows signs of dying down, there's a new development."

Travers looked at her. "What's she done now?"

Ben merely took the *Washington Herald* and ran down the front page article:

Frederic Barnes, brother of Philip J. Barnes, whose mysterious death is being probed by DC police, said he suspected foul play. "I don't know what's going on up there," he said, via an exclusive telephone interview from Sarasota, Fla. "I don't take much interest in politics. But, one thing I know. My brother was a God-fearing man. Even if he had troubles, he would keep his faith in Jesus Christ to help him find the way . . ."

"I see what you mean, Madge," said Ben, abandoning the page 18 follow-up. "The police asked all the rest of us to shut up, and I suppose they asked Mrs. Barnes, too."

"But they can't gag a retired plumber in Florida," said Doug.

Ben stood up and stretched. "Karen Jenks and retired

74

plumbers make a powerful combination. Not to speak of her anarchist pals. Oh well. Madge, I'm going over to have a talk with Val Oakes. Doug, try to get some of that material on soybean prices together for me, will you?"

Madge accompanied him to her desk.

"By the way, Mr. Safford, you won't forget Sweden, will you?"

"Sweden?" he repeated, momentarily lost. "Is that tonight?"

It was tonight. Firmly, Ben looked on the bright side. "Well, here's one evening I won't spend worrying about Nuevador or Karen Jenks."

This, it turned out, was another error.

Ben's congressional district in Ohio did not contain the ethnic diversity that kept so many of his colleagues hopping from Tel Aviv to Rome to Dublin. Most of Ben's mail concerned domestic matters. In fact, Ben sometimes suspected that Newburg's interest in international relations was exclusively confined to the price of imported Scotch and Volkswagens.

But in its small way, Newburg was part of the great American melting pot. There was Nick Diangikes who had started out with Nick's Home Cooking on Center Street in 1921. Today he and three sons owned the Newburg Dining Room on Lincolnville Road, the White Pillars Steak House and were currently constructing a 98-unit motel out on Reservoir Road. There was Ling So Ku, still operating the Newburg Hand Laundry. There were Gattos, and Copellos, Bermans and Levines, Wasclesckis and Metcheks.

And there were Gustaffsons, Holgrens and Pedersons. Ben's own brother-in-law ("Biggest Ford Dealer in Southern Ohio") was the grandson of one of those Swedish immigrants who had come to the new world to find fertile farmland in southern Ohio, as well as Minnesota.

So, later that evening, Ben found himself mounting the

great stairs leading to the ballroom of the Swedish Embassy. Formal attire, and his usual struggles with the tie, had left him feeling disgruntled, but he had to admit that things could be worse. Nobody was asking him to assume foolish poses. No, he was simply going to be photographed with the Ambassador; the photograph, thanks to his sister Janet's thoroughness, would appear where it would do the most good. It would also earn him a tart comment. Janet always claimed that he looked disgraceful at the best of times, and drunk in a tuxedo.

"Ah, Mr. Congressman."

The Ambassador smiled broadly during their brief exchange while the flashbulbs exploded. Ben left the receiving line, accepted champagne, and gazed around the ballroom of the Embassy. Since he had arrived early, the room was not yet the solid wall of people it would soon become. There were, however, enough social lions to satisfy the scalphunters. Turbans and robes, Supreme Court justices, an astronaut, and several lady columnists who wrote endlessly about the glitter of the Washington scene.

"Mr. Safford!" It was Quentin Fels, from the Sears Foundation. He was not looking well. "Have they been after you?" he asked, almost like a hunted man.

Ben was momentarily confused. "You mean the police?" he asked hesitantly.

Fels winced, but that was what he meant.

"It's ridiculous," he said waspishly, "people like us don't commit murders. Why don't they check up on that Gallagher? He's a vicious hoodlum—if ever I saw one."

Ben pointed out that Russ Gallagher had not been present when Philip Barnes was murdered.

"How do we know?" Fels snapped back. "That Jenks girl has him in her office all the time. For that matter, why don't the police go after Barnes' wife? Or the people he worked with? They're the sort of people who would have a reason to kill him. Instead, they're wasting their time hounding me!"

Fels was a twister, Ben thought, even when things were going well. When trouble started, he instinctively looked for a whipping boy.

"It will all blow over," Ben said. This was about as much comfort as he was willing to offer Fels.

Fels didn't think much of it. He sounded venomous. "That's easy enough for you to say, Mr. Congressman. They're not persecuting you. Do you realize that they're grilling every single one of us who has visited Nuevador? Do you realize—"

Ben had no intention of prolonging this and he knew a good way to bring it to a halt. "I didn't know you have been in Nuevador recently, Fels. You weren't there when Mrs. Jenks got into difficulty, were you?"

Quentin Fels went white to his lips. He opened his mouth, then shut it.

"Have some champagne," said Ben genially as a passing waiter paused near them.

The hand Fels extended was shaking. "I was in Nuevador a full month before the cathedral incident," he said forcefully.

"Oh really?"

"Yes, really!" Fels snarled. "If you'll pardon me . . ."

Sipping champagne, Ben watched Fels stride away. He seemed to be feeling the strain rather badly, but then, presumably the Sears Foundation did not normally require its executives to bear heavy burdens. It asked only administrative competence.

"I wonder what he was administering in Nuevador?" Ben asked himself although he already knew the answer. Quentin Fels would have visited Nuevador to supervise the Sears Scholars there.

It might have left him with time on his hands, Ben thought.

Finishing his drink, he decided that he was getting as bad as Mrs. Jenks. Suspicious of everything and everyone.

Thoughtfully, Safford began circling the ballroom. As he munched a stuffed celery, he kept one eye on Quentin Fels. Fels, he was not surprised to see, had buttonholed a presidential adviser and was talking furiously. Ben thought he could guess what the talk was about.

A touch on his elbow, light as a feather, claimed his attention. While he had been watching Fels, someone had been watching him.

"Congressman Safford," breathed Señora Luisa Montoya.

In a room of splendidly dressed women, she was radiant, half-empress and half-courtesan. Raven hair framed her bold classic features; the Montoya rubies gleamed against creamy shoulders. But a black chiffon gown, slashed to the waist and caught there by a jeweled buckle, exultantly proclaimed her deep-bosomed splendor.

"Good evening, Señora," said Ben Safford with more caution than usual.

It was no idle encounter.

"I am happy to have this chance to speak with you," Señora Montoya began. "Especially in view of the unfortunate publicity that is being created by Mrs. Jenks."

Was this going to be another appeal to gag Karen, Ben wondered.

"I am, as you know, a good friend of the United States," continued Señora Montoya, moving a step closer. She wore a rich, musky perfume. "Even in such dark days as these, good friends can help minimize the difficulties between our countries. I wish you to know, Congressman Safford, that I have helped persuade our ambassador to postpone any protests about delays in TASA shipments to Nuevador. I have urged my friends at home to counsel moderation. We shall use our influence to keep Mrs. Jenks in perspective. Nuevador, too, has its hot-headed young students."

Ben, no lady's man at best, was out of his depth. "I'm sure you've been very helpful," he responded.

But Señora Montoya was not finished with him. In a peculiarly intimate voice, she said:

"I had hoped, Congressman Safford, that those who think as we do might cooperate. You and I, for example, would be more effective if we consulted informally with each other in emergencies—without having to be constrained by official channels . . ."

Señora Montoya might be enigmatic, but many pressure groups had tried to recruit Ben into their ranks before. The lady was not into her second sentence before Ben saw the desirability of terminating this tête-à-tête. Unobtrusively he searched for assistance. His luck was in; not far away, talking to strangers, were Carl and Willa Zimmerman. Even better, they recognized an SOS when they saw one.

Within seconds, Willa Zimmerman had swept up and was saying: "Señora Montoya! Just the woman Raoul d'Herbeville has been begging me to introduce him to. Raoul has just come to his embassy here . . ."

She burbled on, while Ben looked at her with affection and relief. Willa was a breath of fresh air: plump, childishly buoyant, and sunny-tempered. Next to Luisa Montoya, whom she was bearing irresistibly away, she looked unsophisticated. But Willa, Ben thought on a wave of gratitude, was too interested in life to care much about clothes.

"We saw the señora stalking you, Ben," Carl murmured as the two men followed. "What does she want?"

"She's trying to bypass Olivera, I think," Ben replied. "Tell me, is he pulling the same stunt?"

"There hasn't been a word out of him. Olivera's playing his cards close to his chest." Zimmerman was pensive. "And that's pretty damned suspicious in itself."

Ben left the Zimmermans with Señora Montoya and her admirers. He had had enough socializing for one night. He ducked out the entrance, hurried downstairs and was collecting his topcoat when a man emerging from another door accidentally jostled him.

"Perdone . . . ah, Mr. Safford."

"Good evening, Dr. Olivera," said Safford, cursing his luck. Three hundred guests—and he had to bump into a Nuevadorian! To forestall conversation, he went on, "I'm just leaving."

But Olivera too was departing. And, it subsequently developed, going in the same direction. He suggested that they join forces.

Whatever diplomacy you find in the world today, Ben reflected irritably, is not in the diplomatic corps.

"A splendid reception," he said heartily as they stepped out onto Kalorama Road, hazy in a fine mist.

But if Manuel Olivera was not talking to the State Department, he was to Ben Safford.

"You have seen the latest reports from Nuevador?" he asked in that harsh voice. "There are reports that some army units are threatening to mutiny against the government."

"I am sorry to hear it," said Ben. His companion was a slow walker; he began to fear the length of their exchange.

"Sorry!" said Olivera with a flash of his old spirit. "Sorry! The Vallonistas are like hawks—waiting, waiting, waiting! They are ready to strike, to get back into power!"

The steady drizzle made it difficult for them to see each other. Perhaps this encouraged Olivera to continue.

"Do you know what that means?" he cried. "Can you imagine what Nuevador is like when the Vallons rule? When the Montoyas control the army? When these respectable friends of America have power? Do you know? Do you know what the prisons were like—with professors and students, with doctors and women treated like animals? Do you know of the murders in Puerto Montecigalpa—with soldiers at midnight, then machine guns for anybody who dared criticize the regime? Do you know of newspapers forced to lie? Of courts that were a mockery? All of this—this is what the great friends of America meant to Nuevador!"

Ben Safford could not match the anguished sincerity of the shrouded figure trudging beside him. He tried to be honest.

"I don't deny that there are some legitimate reasons for your anti-Americanism. We've made mistakes in the past. We'll probably make them in the future. But, look at the situation right now. Your friends are in power—and their biggest difficulty is their lack of strong, popular support. But that's Nuevador's problem—not ours. You'd be the first to yell bloody murder if we butted in. So, you're using anti-Americanism to get the popularity you don't have—and, meanwhile, this country is still shipping you economic aid. Would you behave as well?"

There was a long silence. They passed a shadowy amorous couple. When he spoke, Olivera's passion was spent. He sounded morose.

"There is fear that the CIA is behind this trouble. The Jenks woman—everything."

Ben Safford felt, rather than saw, the accompanying gesture.

"You've been in Washington long enough to know that there are always rumors about the CIA," he said. "I can assure you that I, for one, have had no intimation that they are involved. My own guess would be that they're still trying to figure out what's happening. That's just for what it's worth."

His caution had cost him his audience.

Olivera's voice came from the mist. "But there must be something behind all this. Karen Jenks did not come to Nuevador by accident. The incident at the cathedral must have been arranged. By America—or by her lackeys."

Safford could strike too. "I've heard it suggested that

you and your party arranged the whole thing in order to embarrass the Montoyas."

"The Montoyas!" said that triumphant, slightly mad voice. "It is time they looked like fools. The Montoyas—they think of themselves as our royalty. Do not think the señora is not watched. She is buying equipment and sending it back to her estancia, you know! But I am checking! Let her try to smuggle goods into Nuevador—or let her try to ship guns— and I, Manuel Olivera, will know. I have requisitioned all the order forms. And, if you Americans are working through TASA—if you are helping our enemies—then I will find out . . ."

It dawned on Safford that Manuel Olivera was drunk. "Olivera," he began.

"No," Olivera cried. "I will find out. Do not worry . . ."

Fortunately, they turned the corner to find a taxi stand. Firmly grasping Olivera, who was almost slack, Safford steered him into the first cab. There was no resistance. Ben shut the door, and directed the driver to proceed to the Nuevadorian Embassy.

Then he stood, watching the taillights recede.

Just how drunk had Manuel Olivera been?

Chapter 9

By the time Ben plodded through the mist to the Carlton, he was thoroughly soaked. During this long wet walk home, he had time to ask himself a number of questions. Unfortunately, he did not have the answers. Turning into the hotel, he was ready for a hot shower, a nightcap, and a chance to put Nuevador from his mind. An unpleasant surprise awaited him.

There, at the reception desk, stood a uniformed policeman. He had been speaking to the desk clerk, but at the sound of the doors, he turned.

"Mr. Safford? May I have a few words with you, sir?"

Ben Safford was taken aback. So was the desk clerk.

The policeman courteously waited for his agreement, then, stolidly, accompanied him to one of the plush chairs away from the desk.

"Thank you, sir," he said. "It's a question of where you spent the evening. Just a formality . . ."

"Now, wait a minute!" Ben protested. Then he stopped, gave the officer a brief but comprehensive account of his movements since five o'clock. Only then did he go on with his first natural impulse. "Officer, exactly what is this all about?"

The policeman, who was young, grinned at the self-control that had deferred curiosity. But all he said was, "Sorry, sir. I've got orders . . ."

He left Ben and the desk clerk with dark thoughts between them, returned to headquarters, and placed a radio message.

"Okay," said Captain Rigsby. "That takes care of Safford. Check out every single one of them. Everybody who has had anything to do with the Barnes case. Fedder has the list—and keep me informed."

Rigsby was in a patrol car on a suburban street in Garrett Park, Maryland. The mist that had soaked Ben Safford in the city was a steady pelting rain here. And there was none of the somnolence of Kalorama Road. Two spotlights were trained on a modest split-level house. From other police cars came the jabbering chatter of the police radio. Despite the rain, there were knots of people standing about. Some of them huddled under umbrellas, others wore raincoats over pajamas and nightgowns. There was an ambulance with a revolving blinker pulled into the driveway. Its doors were open.

Rigsby walked up the path to join Captain Lassiter of the Garrett Park force, carefully avoiding two men who were examining long scratch marks on the front door. An area of the stoop had been protected by a tarpaulin that gleamed blackly under the light. Garrett Park was out of Captain Rigsby's jurisdiction, but it was still his baby and Lassiter knew it. The uniformed men examining, measuring and questioning were the local police. "The rest," said Lassiter, "I leave up to you."

Rigsby grunted, and the two police officers went indoors. The living room was crowded. On a faded couch, a blanket covered a half-reclining woman. Two men in white coats hovered over her, while she feverishly clutched a small boy. Nearby at the telephone table, a white-faced twelve-year-old girl was fighting tears; a burly detective clumsily tried to comfort her.

As the officers entered, Howard Creighton stepped forward from the doorway. "Captain," he whispered angrily, "this is no place for these children. I don't know what happened here tonight, but that much is clear. Good Lord, man, Mrs. Barnes is still bleeding! Why don't those two do their job!" He glared at the men in white.

Rigsby glanced at the youngsters. "Like I said, Mr. Creighton, Mike is talking to the sister now. She's coming right over. And the doctor said it would do Mrs. Barnes less harm to wait than to get upset again. She had a pretty bad shock. She doesn't want to go to the hospital until the kids are with their aunt."

"But what happened?" Creighton insisted.

Rigsby and Captain Lassiter exchanged a look. The local man replied. "We still aren't sure. The call came from the neighbors. When we got here, she was still out."

As if on signal, one of the interns spoke up. "You can have a few words with her now, Cap," he said. "Not too long. She's going to fall off to sleep soon . . ."

Both Rigsby and Lassiter moved toward the couch. Howard Creighton was more reluctant. He had already spotted a bowl filled with reddish liquid, together with bloody swabs nearby. But he, too, wanted to learn what had happened.

Captain Rigsby settled into a chair drawn near Mrs. Barnes. The little boy in her arms was half asleep. Rigsby kept his voice very low.

"Now, Mrs. Barnes," he began, "if you're well enough, maybe you could just tell us what happened, while we wait for your sister."

She looked at the circle of men around her, Rigsby in the chair, Lassiter behind him, the doctor keeping a finger

85

on her left wrist. There was wadding taped to her temple, her hair was disheveled, and the flannel bathrobe was old and shabby. But Mrs. Barnes could still fight.

"I will not go to the hospital until Elaine is here to take care of Johnny!"

"No, ma'am," said Rigsby. "We understand that. Your daughter is talking to your sister now."

Almost wildly, Mrs. Barnes looked toward her daughter. Then she closed her eyes again. Rigsby had a shrewd suspicion that she had forgotten about the girl.

Mrs. Barnes spoke: "It is the mercy of the Lord that we weren't all murdered!"

Rigsby glanced at the doctor who nodded encouragingly. "Now, Mrs. Barnes, can you just start at the beginning? You were all asleep."

"Yes," she replied dully. "We were all in bed by ten-thirty."

"And there hadn't been anything to disturb you during the evening?"

She looked at him blankly and he expanded: "Telephone calls or visitors?"

"Why, no," said Mrs. Barnes. "It was an ordinary evening. After dinner, Reverend Pleydell and Mrs. Pleydell came by to bring me a few words of comfort. I don't know if you realize that I've just lost my husband?"

Rigsby nodded but said nothing.

"He's gone to a better world," said Mrs. Barnes, tears beginning to steal unheeded down her cheeks. "I know that—but I appreciated the visit. Then, after we had read Corinthians together, they left. I made a cup of tea and went to bed."

And that was the last that Mrs. Barnes knew until she was awakened by some noise. Glancing at the clock, she saw it was twelve-thirty.

"And you went downstairs? Alone?" Howard Creighton was startled. "Didn't you think that was dangerous?"

The police officers scowled at him, but he had not upset Mrs. Barnes.

"My faith is in the Lord," she said. "He provides." She fell silent, then went on, "Anyway, I thought it was the thermostat. Perhaps, in all my troubles, I had forgotten to turn it down. My husband was putting in a new heating system with an automatic thermostat—" This reminder of the domestic plans she had shared with her husband brought tears.

Creighton made an indistinct noise in his throat, but Lassiter, standing beside him, clutched his arm to ensure silence.

"So you went downstairs . . ." Rigsby prompted.

"Yes," Mrs. Barnes said obediently. "The thermostat is in the hallway that leads to the garage, and to my husband's study. I was just reaching for it, when I saw a line of light under the study door. I didn't have time to do anything, I didn't even have time to think. The door opened, and this creature stood there! He had something in his hand—" She shook her head, then winced in pain. The doctor leaned forward for a moment, but she continued: "After that, I don't remember anything else until you were all here. But when I woke up, Johnny was crying . . ."

She looked down at the little boy now sleeping the sleep of total exhaustion and stroked his corn-colored hair with her free hand.

"Yes, ma'am. That was terrible." Rigsby was sympathetic. "As near as we can figure out, he heard you fall and came down. That brought your daughter down and, between them, they made enough noise to rouse the neighbors."

"Jesus loves the little children," said Mrs. Barnes tearfully. "He saved Johnny from that terrible man."

Rigsby gritted his teeth and pushed on. "Are you sure it was a man?"

She stared at him without comprehension. Howard Creighton checked an unguarded exclamation. The doctor began to look concerned.

"Of course it was a man!" said Mrs. Barnes. But there was doubt in her face. "No woman would have . . . but there was something over his face. A stocking, I suppose. I thought he was a man. But I don't know, I don't know!"

Rigsby ignored the doctor's frown and said quickly, "Mrs. Barnes, one more thing. Are you sure he was alone?"

She was tiring rapidly now. Her voice dropped almost to a murmur. "It's so hard to remember. There was just the flashlight. I don't know. I don't know . . ."

Her voice trailed away. The intern straightened but Rigsby forestalled him.

"OK, doc, that's all." He rose, looked down at Mrs. Barnes compassionately, and stepped out of the room into the hallway.

"Not much to go on," said Lassiter, stopping to confer with a uniformed man just coming in.

Howard Creighton had jammed his hands deep into his pockets.

Rigsby looked at him. "The reason we called you, Mr. Creighton, is simple. We think this is tied in with Phil Barnes' murder."

Creighton was shaken. He did not look up. "I'm glad you did," he muttered. "God, that poor woman—"

"This joker broke into the house, made straight for Barnes' study and was going through the files when Mrs. Barnes interrupted him."

"But what could be in Phil Barnes' files?" Creighton demanded.

Rigsby and Lassiter looked at him. "That's what we want to know. There seems to be the usual personal stuff—but nobody's going to break in to get that. Then, there's some stuff from the TASA office—"

Howard Creighton expelled an exasperated breath. "Oh for crissake!" he said wearily. "If Phil Barnes had any

88

TASA stuff here, it was just routine business he was checking over. You'd better send it back to the office—" He broke off and looked at the police officers. "Oh for God's sake," he repeated helplessly.

Rigsby seemed to understand this. "I know how you feel. But there's been a lot of talk, lately, about TASA—"

"That damned Jenks girl," Creighton growled.

"Don't get me wrong," Rigsby said. "The police don't take notice of what some crazy kid says. We leave that to the politicians. But, Creighton, Barnes did work for you—and he was murdered! Now his house is broken into, that poor woman inside attacked! I want you to look over this TASA stuff for us, and tell us exactly what it is . . ."

Creighton followed him down the short hallway. The thermostat was there on the wall and, beneath it, a large brown stain, still muddy and viscous on the carpeting.

"Don't go inside yet," Rigsby cautioned. "Just stay here for a minute. It's clear enough what the guy was after."

Philip Barnes' study was small. There was a desk on one wall and a tall file cabinet on the opposite side. All the drawers were pulled out and some folders lay on the floor. A fingerprint man was carefully dusting them.

"Went straight for the files," Lassiter murmured. "Jim's about finished."

Creighton stepped back, and nearly tripped over a pile of lumber.

"Watch it," said Lassiter. "They're putting in a recreation room and a bathroom downstairs. I guess they stopped work for the funeral. We're going to check out the workmen. But, if the newspapers are halfway right . . ."

Creighton was silent. He remained silent when Captain Rigsby handed him several folders to look over. He looked through them quickly and said:

"Just what I told you! These are nothing but old invoices Phil was checking over. There's nothing here of any interest to anyone! Certainly no reason for a burglary."

When neither policeman answered, Creighton went on: "Look, I've read the papers as well as you have. That Jenks kid doesn't know what she's talking about. There's nothing at TASA, there was nothing in Phil's work that could have anything to do with his murder. This whole damned thing is a figment of that girl's neurotic imagination."

"Phil Barnes' murder wasn't," said Rigsby unemotionally. "And somebody broke in here tonight to look for something—and he was willing to club down an innocent woman for it. That's not imagination, Mr. Creighton."

"For all I know," said Howard Creighton furiously, "that crazy kid did it all herself—just for more publicity."

"That's not a possibility we're overlooking," said Captain Rigsby.

He did not add one further piece of information. A rapid police search for the whereabouts of everybody connected with the Barnes murder had turned up only one person missing. That person was Karen Kimball Jenks.

Chapter 10

By seven o'clock the next morning, Ben Safford knew what had happened at the Barnes house. When he reached his office, he learned one thing further: Karen Jenks was still missing.

Jolted, Safford voiced his first thought: "No, I don't know where she is—but, my God, Rigsby, you don't think a girl ransacked that house and clubbed Mrs. Barnes!"

"She's a good-sized girl," said the phone calmly, "and that kid Gallagher would do anything. We ran him down at a coffeehouse in Georgetown, but he doesn't have much of a story for how he spent the evening. And he can't, or he won't, tell us where the Jenks girl is now."

Ben exchanged a worried look with Doug Travers, who was on the extension. After promising to inform Rigsby if Karen Jenks turned up, he decided he could ask some questions. "What about everybody else? Are they in the clear?"

Rigsby was evasive. "There are some loose ends," he replied. "It isn't easy for most people to produce an alibi for twelve-thirty at night. Unless they're married. And we don't really trust wives."

Whose wife was he thinking of, Ben wondered. Aloud, he said he was pleased to hear that there were other suspects.

"We've got open minds, Mr. Congressman," the phone replied. "But it's kind of funny—Mrs. Jenks is the only one who's missing. And no one seems to know where she is."

"You're not going to put out an official call for her, are you?" asked Ben, alarmed.

The answer was not reassuring. "Not yet," said Rigsby. "Not yet."

After he hung up, Ben looked wordlessly at Doug Travers. Then: "Well, it could be worse," he said. "They still think the field is wide open."

"Yeah," said Travers.

Ben ignored the tone. "But I wonder what Phil Barnes was keeping under wraps? There must have been a reason for that burglary."

"Not to mention that murder," Travers added.

There was another uncomfortable silence. Ben roused himself. "Well, whatever it is, it's somebody else's baby. We've got to get some work done around here—that's why we came in on a Saturday."

Travers headed for his own office. Ben himself was going to put in four hours of dictation. That should go a long way toward clearing the decks. Ben had a strong feeling that it was now or never.

After his usual preliminary struggle with the tape recorder, he got through a long letter to Roy Hacket, one of his Newburg supporters. He outlined an evasive reply to Mrs. Dorothy Bandolier, who regularly complained about U.S. gun laws, taxes, and foreign policy. Mrs. Bandolier was a one-woman explanation for Ben's feelings about those who urge people to write their congressmen.

After Ben had dealt with Mrs. Bandolier, he picked up

92

letter number three and discovered the first tentacles of political conspiracy.

It was from Justin F. Gebhard who was, as the letterhead proclaimed, executive vice-president of Gebhard & Gebhard. Gebhard & Gebhard, Ben knew, not only manufactured precision instruments in a large modern factory, they made substantial contributions to the Newburg Republican organization. Ben read carefully, although the first sentence told the story:

Dear Mr. Congressman,

According to the *Newburg News*, you have been dealing with TASA in connection with certain recent events. It occurred to us . . .

What had occurred to Gebhard & Gebhard was that they wanted to sell their product to TASA. "Annual TASA purchases of metering devices amount to seven million dollars. If Gebhard & Gebhard can submit a bid, the business would be a big boost for the local economy, in terms of payroll and jobs. Sincerely yours . . ."

Under his breath, Ben Safford damned the Gebhards. This was their attempt to pull a fast one. Ben's opposition in the November election would be Lewis E. Frome, husband of a Gebhard daughter. The Gebhards knew that a Democratic congressman was not likely to succeed where a Republican senator had already failed. So here was a real sleeper. Ben could hear Frome nasally declaiming: ". . . my opponent spends time worrying about hippies, but doesn't care about Newburg business and Newburg working people. When I'm elected to Congress, I'll . . ."

"Oh, no, you won't, buster!" Ben muttered, reaching for the phone.

The long shot paid off. An aggrieved voice told Congressman Safford that Mr. Creighton was in the office. Ben requested an early afternoon appointment. Then, just before he rang off, the voice gave him further information:

"We're *all* on a six-day week here."

It did not sound as if TASA were a happy ship.

TASA, Technical Assistance to South America, was housed at the other end of Constitution Avenue. The guard who checked Ben's name against a list and phoned for Creighton's secretary was surly.

The trim young woman with a Texan accent who promptly appeared was also mutinous.

"Mr. Creighton is working in Mr. Barnes' office. I might just as well take you right over to him."

She flounced ahead, down an aisle formed by rows of desks in the building-wide room. The desks were occupied by young girls at typewriters, with an occasional young man bending over to give instructions. Shirtsleeves and subdued frenzy characterized the men; the girls were uniformly sulky.

Safford and his guide had come to the far end of the room. Without ceremony, she opened a door:

"Congressman Safford," she announced.

Howard Creighton looked up in surprise. He was at a desk, poring over a large pile of papers. "Why . . ."

"I have to go back to check the 1968 price list," the young woman announced defiantly. With a whirl of red skirt, she disappeared.

Creighton, smiling wryly, rose to shake Safford's hand. "Might as well settle down here since you've come the distance, Mr. Congressman."

Ben sat. "Maybe your girl doesn't trust me enough to leave me alone in your office."

Wearily Creighton shook his head. "You know how it is. Working on Saturday burns them up. And we're in a helluva mess, with shipments backpiling. At the moment, TASA morale is falling fast . . ."

94

Safford found himself wondering about Creighton's morale. It was hard to tell. Creighton was certainly haggard, with dark circled eyes. On the other hand, he was here, trying to keep TASA functioning during a crisis. That argued a certain stability.

"How are things going?" Ben asked cautiously.

Creighton was frank. "They couldn't be worse."

"Is this all because of Barnes' murder?" Safford asked bluntly.

With mute frustration, Creighton slammed a big hand down on the desk. "Damned if I know! Hell, after last night, I'd be crazy to say anything. I don't understand what the hell is going on!"

"You're not the only one," Ben told him.

Creighton nodded. "I know," he said. "Still, until somebody gives me some hard facts, I say that what's bitching us up here is the breakdown of our routine. Everything's snowballed into a king-size mess."

Ben pointed out that it had started with Barnes.

Creighton was almost eager to agree. "I never denied that losing Phil was what started everything—but where that ties up with his getting killed, or his house getting burgled . . ."

He shrugged his shoulders in perplexity, and Ben suddenly recalled Manuel Olivera's insinuations about TASA. He thought for a moment, then raised a point that had been bothering him. "Creighton, I know Barnes was one of your key men. But I still don't see how an agency as big as TASA can get knocked for a loop when one man— any man—is removed. After all, people resign, they take annual leave, they get sick, they die . . ."

Creighton interrupted. "You're absolutely right, although we are understaffed. But the situation is really more complicated. First of all, Phil really was a take-charge guy when it came to making our purchases, assembling our monthly shipments and making sure they left our warehouse

95

on time. You know we've got a big stock inventory over there in Maryland. Phil kept it running like clockwork."

Olivera, of course, would say that conspiracy required efficiency. Ben listened as Creighton went on:

"So when Phil was knocked out of the picture, things didn't move so smoothly. Some confusion was only to be expected. Three or four of us have had to move in and take over his job—and naturally we're not so hot at it. We need somebody to take over full time."

"It sounds as if you're going to have to hire Superman," Ben said.

"No," Creighton was serious. "Phil's job was tough, but it wasn't impossible. Hell, at first we managed to keep everything on schedule, except for that one Nuevadorian load. That's gone sour, I admit, but still it's not a bad record. No, the real trouble came from outside."

Ben braced himself for another indictment of Karen Jenks. It did not come.

Creighton continued: "First of all, the Nuevadorians started complaining. They've been on the phone every day. They've tied us up in conferences for hours. They want reports and explanations. Why don't we ship? What are we trying to hide? Why can't we explain the delay? And worse!"

So, Dr. Olivera was not playing it as cool as Carl Zimmerman thought. Hands-off in public, Ben reflected, didn't preclude behind-the-scene pressure.

"So, we've explained," said Creighton savagely, "but that doesn't satisfy that SOB Olivera. Hell, nothing would. He's out for blood. He thinks he's got us by the short hairs. God, if it weren't for the fact that Señora Montoya has pull with the Ambassador—and she's got some understanding of this situation—we'd be tied up in knots. The Ambassador is still saying that he understands our difficulties and telling us to take our time. Of course, he

96

wants action too. But at least he's not accusing us of smuggling Marines in with farm equipment!"

"Nuevador is certainly a divided country," Ben mused aloud.

With unmistakable and venomous sincerity, Howard Creighton said, "I'm so goddam fed up with *all* Nuevadorians—" He broke off, and continued more temperately: "Anyway, that's what started the ball rolling. We've had every single TASA aid country demanding a program review. We've been preparing statements for eighteen countries, explaining what we ship, how we're not military, what our safeguards are. We have crackpots claiming that we're doing espionage work—and we've got to answer them! Do you know what we're doing today?"

Ben did not.

"We're preparing an itemized list of every single item of aid we've shipped to Nuevador for the last three years. Do you understand what that means? That's thousands of farm machines, drills, irrigation pipes, tractors, replacement parts—together with prices, the supplying firms, dates. Well, we can do it—but it's taking time. So, we're running into delays on our current shipments—and that's starting the whole vicious circle going. I've got the Brazilians on my neck later today."

Ben recalled Dr. Olivera's plan of action.

"Tell me," he said cautiously. "Are you agreeing to do all this for Manuel Olivera?"

Creighton stared. "Hell, no! I wouldn't do this for anybody, if I didn't have to. But I've got orders from the State Department."

Lips clamped shut told Ben that nothing short of the State Department—and possibly higher authority—could have pried detailed TASA information about Nuevador shipments from Howard Creighton. Ben could not blame him.

"I'm a little ashamed to be bothering you now," he said

aloud. "My problem is peanuts, compared to yours. I'd like to know TASA's reasons for keeping Gebhard & Gebhard off the approved list . . ."

Howard Creighton was immediately transformed into a competent official.

"Gebhard & Gebhard?" he repeated, rumpling his shock of graying hair. "Oh, the meter and gauge people. Out in your bailiwick, are they? Well, if they've applied, we'll have a report on them. I guess we'll have to go back to my office, after all."

Without delay, Safford was again charging down the desk-lined aisle. Creighton, he observed, had a greeting for several subordinates. In smooth seas, Ben guessed, Creighton would be rated a good, easygoing top man, with none of the pompousness that is the curse of many Washington agencies. Right now, it was rough going for all concerned at TASA.

"No, I'm all in favor of giving out as much TASA information as we can," Creighton said when Milly produced a file. "What burns me, is having to play ball with anti-American bastards like Olivera. But something that makes people understand how TASA operates, something to make people trust us—that's different. Milly!"—this was a bellow —"there's nothing here."

"Try the pending file," she replied pertly, depositing a new folder on his desk.

Creighton exchanged an amused look with Safford and started checking again. He moved his lips slightly as he read. Then: "Here they are! Well, you're in luck, Mr. Safford. Next Friday, Gebhard & Gebhard—and fifteen other firms—are going to be added to the approved list. Official announcement release is due on Friday. Why don't you jump the gun?"

Safford was already planning a private hint. It turned out that Creighton was thinking of a public announcement. Ben asked if this might not cause a ruckus.

Creighton grinned. "With our current problems we'll never notice." Abruptly he turned almost somber. "And here at TASA we need friends these days."

As he drove back to his office, Safford indulged in several pleasant visions.

One was the announcement in tomorrow's *Newburg News:*

Congressman Benton Safford today announced that Gebhard & Gebhard has been given the opportunity to bid on important government contracts. "My concern," said Congressman Safford, "is for Newburg jobs, income and business . . ."

Another was the response of the assorted Gebhards, and Miss Gebhard's husband, Lewis Frome, Republican candidate for Congressman from Ohio's fiftieth district.

Still another was a letter:

Dear Gebhard:
  I was only sorry you had not brought this matter to my attention earlier . . .

And, perhaps best of all, the reaction of Senator Duane Halsey (R., Ohio), a relic of another century whose boast that he served all the folks of Ohio rested on a highly restrictive definition of folks.

Yet, obtruding through his satisfaction was an insistent, deepening disquiet. And Douglas Travers did nothing to dispel it when he reported that there had been three more calls from the Washington, D.C. police. And there was still no sign of Karen Jenks.

Chapter 11

Sunday was no day of rest for Ben Safford, or his staff, either. Not while the police were scouring Washington for Karen Jenks, not while Philip Barnes' murder was still unsolved, and not while congressional work was piling up. Ben, Madge, and Doug were at their desks. Safford was deep in a mountain of correspondence, jotting brief notes to indicate the gist of a reply or further action, when he was interrupted in the middle of the afternoon by a telephone call from his sister, Janet. She reported that the *Newburg News* had done him proud with Gebhard & Gebhard.

"Thank God," Ben said briefly. "It's time I got some publicity that wasn't connected with the Jenks mess."

There was a pause.

"I don't know about that, Ben," Janet finally said. "Everybody in Newburg is on Karen Jenks' side."

"Most of them haven't met her. They can afford to be on her side."

His sister simply ignored this and continued reflectively:

"You know, it might not be a bad idea if you showed up here with her."

Janet was more than an older sister; she was Ben's year-round campaign manager in Newburg. He had a healthy respect for her detailed knowledge of Newburg's people, problems and opinions. But he did not always agree with her.

"My God, Janet, have you gone crazy? You don't know Karen Jenks. She's wild, she's egocentric, and generally hell on wheels!"

"Ben," was the firm reply, "Newburg has a younger generation, too. They're all like that now."

Ben had scarcely put down the receiver when Doug Travers marched into the office.

"Karen's coming back," he announced.

"Where the hell has she been?" Safford demanded.

"Maureen didn't know." Seeing the question on Safford's face, Doug hastily explained Maureen. "Anyway, Maureen says Karen called her this afternoon, claiming she just read about Mrs. Barnes in the paper today. She's flying back to Washington tomorrow morning. She told Maureen to set up an appointment with Captain Rigsby."

"Then our troubles are about to begin," said Ben, thinking rapidly. There was no use speculating about where Karen had gone, or what she had been doing. Presumably she would tell them tomorrow—if she was still at large.

"Doug," he said, "I think you'd better be there when Rigsby talks to her."

Doug was startled. "But what if Rigsby won't go along—?"

Safford was emphatic. "Then I want you right outside the door! That girl can't recognize real danger. She probably thinks she's going to lay down the law to Rigsby and the police. It's never occurred to her that she's the one who's on the spot right now."

"And high time!" Doug was just as emphatic. "Let's hope it shakes her up!"

It did.

"Do you know what he was getting at?" Karen demanded, storming out of Rigsby's office the next morning. "He suspected *me* of blackjacking Mrs. Barnes!"

"Well, what did you expect?" Doug Travers was unsympathetic as he rose from the bench where he had been waiting. "You've been running around like a maniac, threatening to tear the place apart. Now, somebody makes a start on the job, and you go into the outraged-innocent bit because the police look your way."

"Try to use what little brain you've got!" she spat. "I said there ought to be an investigation. That doesn't mean breaking into people's homes and cracking skulls!"

"But do you know the difference?" he countered. "I haven't seen you shedding tears for Philip Barnes, and he had every bone in his body cracked."

"That wasn't the same!"

"Sure, it wasn't. The police didn't put out a call for you and your tough boyfriend."

"That wasn't what I meant, and he isn't my boyfriend." Before Doug could interrupt, Karen swept on. "I suppose it is unfeeling, but when a man is dead he isn't around reacting to what's happened to him. But Mrs. Barnes is here, and she looks terrible! They've shaved the side of her head and put in stitches. And she's worried about her little boy. I think it's awful!"

Doug looked at her curiously. "How do you know what Mrs. Barnes looks like?"

"Because I went to see her in the hospital." Karen was swift to sense an advantage. "I suppose you're too busy being a professional bleeding heart for that sort of thing."

"Do you mean to tell me you went straight from the

airport to pay a visit of condolence?" His skepticism was not complimentary.

As Ben Safford could have told him, dishonesty was not one of Karen's faults. Tempted for a moment, she resisted and broke into an impish grin.

"No. I wanted the score before I saw Captain Rigsby."

Doug eyed her suspiciously before breaking into a grin himself. "That wasn't a bad idea."

Karen sobered instantly. "But I didn't realize she'd look that way. And her sister came in while I was there; she says the little boy is still afraid to be left alone. Do you realize that an experience like that can affect him for life?"

Doug emitted a sympathetic grunt but said only: "At least, there's one good thing. You took a plane out of Washington at nine o'clock Friday night and spent the evening with your parents. What I don't understand, is why nobody knew where you were."

"I don't see why you're making a production out of it. I go home every week end."

"Maureen told me you go away every week end, but she thought it was to New York."

Karen became haughty.

"Maureen is not my father confessor!"

"Russ Gallagher didn't know either," Doug persisted. "After all, if you make a habit of it—"

"Oh, for God's sake!" Karen snapped, exasperated. "Use your head! I am not broadcasting the fact that I spend every week end with my son."

"Your son?" Doug had forgotten her child.

"My son. A little boy, just like Mrs. Barnes' little boy."

Doug was at a loss. He did not think of Karen as a mother. What did she do on these visits to Newburg, Ohio? Did she change her son's diapers and heat his bottles? If so, there was a Karen he did not know. But he thought he understood why she chose to keep her two lives separate.

She did not wish to continue the subject.

"But that is none of Russ's business and none of yours," she said distantly. "Now what is this meeting you're dragging me to? I'm sick and tired of meetings."

"As soon as Zimmerman heard you'd be back in town today, he set up a conference over at State," Doug explained. "Everybody concerned in the TASA deal is going to be there. Congressman Safford told me to bring you along when the police were through with us."

"Why didn't you tell me right away?"

"I thought you might want to hang around while the police checked out Gallagher's alibi." Doug knew what he was doing.

"Russ can take care of himself," she said without interest. "But I'm glad to see that I've finally goosed the State Department into getting off its duff and doing what it's paid for."

"Yeah. A great victory," Doug said tersely. "Only I don't care much for your methods."

Karen looked at him suspiciously. Captain Rigsby's methods had left their mark after all. She was beginning to look before she leaped.

"Why not?"

"You've racked up a great score so far. One corpse and one hospital case."

Karen's eyes widened.

But she had not really changed very much, as Ben Safford discovered when Doug Travers steered her into Carl Zimmerman's office an hour later.

"Almost the same cast," she said looking at the gathering. "I wonder who'll go out the window this time."

Forcefully, Travers thrust her into a chair. Carl Zimmerman said something under his breath, but Dr. Olivera ignored the newcomers.

"I particularly requested the presence of Mr. Creighton,"

he said, resuming the complaint he had been voicing before Doug and Karen joined the meeting.

Zimmerman glanced irritably at Ben Safford and Quentin Fels who were sitting opposite him. When he turned back to Olivera, he was not cordial. "I know you did, Dr. Olivera. And he has been invited to join us. He is simply late . . ."

Olivera leaned back with a thin smile while Zimmerman went on: "My superiors have decided to cooperate with you, Dr. Olivera, but we wish to be sure that the government of Nuevador is . . . er . . . adequately represented. Señora Montoya will also be joining us."

That got rid of the smile. Quentin Fels, who had been nervously drumming his fingers on the conference table, burst into speech. "Well, I, for one, don't see what the purpose of all this is. First of all, Mr. Zimmerman, I didn't realize that the State Department was running errands for every Tom, Dick or Harry. Furthermore, I don't see what you hope to accomplish . . ."

Contemptuously, Dr. Olivera cut in: "There is excellent reason for a study of TASA's activities in Nuevador. I had hoped its conduct would be tactful, but since Mr. Zimmerman has seen fit to make this impossible—"

"Now, just a minute!" said Fels loudly. "I understood that we were going to discuss the whole—the whole problem." What the problem was, he left unspecified except for a long, angry look at Karen Jenks.

Olivera was lofty. "The time for such foolishness is over," he said coldly. "I insist that we study the TASA aid program to Nuevador—"

Fels would not be silenced. "*You* insist! I thought Nuevador was represented by an ambassador. How does *he* feel?"

Olivera's eyes glittered. "I speak with the authority of the Foreign Minister of Nuevador," he retorted. "And, Mr. Fels, let me assure you we have ample grounds for making this request. I have here information about all TASA shipments to my country for the last three years." He dug into a briefcase and produced a large clutch of papers. "These must be reviewed. Also, I have obtained documents on private shipments going to Nuevador. And I insist that these, too, be studied."

He looked at his audience. "You understand, we intend to be sure that what went into Nuevador is actually on these lists. You, no doubt, think that Nuevadorian customs can be bribed! But I assure you they have information—"

Quentin Fels was beyond his depth. "What is all this? What's he talking about?"

"Dr. Olivera," Zimmerman said tautly, "is implying that there has been some sort of plot to smuggle goods into Nuevador."

Olivera raised a mocking eyebrow. "I said it was worth study," he said.

"And," Zimmerman continued, "he's implying that TASA is in it. He is also implying that somebody else is involved."

Fels spoke without thinking. "You mean the Montoyas?" he gasped.

Olivera became polite. "Oh, it is true that the Montoyas are very rich. And they import goods for their estate."

"You wouldn't dare repeat this in front of Señora Montoya." Fels told him.

Olivera's white teeth gleamed. "I am willing to repeat anything I have said. Better yet, I am willing to have Mr. Zimmerman repeat it—"

Zimmerman shifted angrily but before he could comment, the door opened and his secretary ushered in Howard Creighton. Creighton was rumpled and red-eyed, and his greeting was partly a gesture of weariness. Quentin Fels gave no one an opportunity to speak.

"Well, I for one think this is disgraceful," he sputtered. "And you will too, Creighton. Do you realize that this is not a meeting to discuss the current crisis? Not at all.

It seems to be some idea of Dr. Olivera's about an investigation of TASA aid! And for some reason, Mr. Zimmerman has been acting as Olivera's deputy."

This tirade left Howard Creighton puzzled. "I don't get that," he said, lowering himself into a chair. "I thought this was a State Department operation."

"It is," Zimmerman said, as Quentin Fels snorted. "The fact that we have listened to an outside request doesn't change the situation. This is State's responsibility."

Olivera, Ben noticed, was saying nothing. The same could not be said for Karen Jenks.

"It's time somebody took responsibility," she declared. "I don't care about these bureaucratic battles of yours. But I know that TASA aid could stand a lot of looking into."

Creighton peered at her from beneath bushy brows. Ben Safford hastily made his one and only contribution to the afternoon's progress.

"Instead of squabbling," he said, "suppose we try to get started. On a more systematic basis."

Dr. Olivera, at any rate, was not at a loss. "An excellent idea," he said. "My proposal is that we outline an investigation of the entire crisis. This necessarily implies a study of the TASA aid program. Clearly that is central. I suggest that we scrutinize the shipments for three years . . ."

Howard Creighton was still at a loss. "That list you've got there, Doctor. Is that a copy of the one I prepared for the State Department?"

"Yes, it is," Carl Zimmerman spoke before the Nuevadorian replied.

Creighton kept his voice level. "You might have told me what you wanted it for, Carl."

Zimmerman flushed. "I expect we'll have to run off copies for the auditors and everyone else."

For some reason this infuriated Karen Jenks. "Auditors!

What good will they do? You're still trying to brush this under the rug."

Zimmerman was taken aback. "The experts in this sort of thing, Mrs. Jenks, are the auditors."

"What sort of thing?" Karen countered swiftly.

Zimmerman rolled his eyes. "You tell me," he said shortly. "You're the one who's been making accusations in every newspaper in the country."

Doug Travers stirred restively, but Karen lashed back, "I don't have to know all about it. This is the kind of mess you can see by just using your eyes. Who needs auditors? Just go down to the docks in Nuevador—and you'll see thirteen crates as big as this room labeled TASA! And you know what you see two blocks away? You see dirty little black marketeers hawking American aid and making fat profits!"

Howard Creighton exploded. "Oh, for God's sake! I'm sick and tired of this nonsense—" He made a stab at self-control. "Mrs. Jenks, aside from the fact that you don't know what an auditor is—tell me, do you know what TASA aid is?"

This was unexpected. Karen frowned. "It's economic aid to South America," she said. "Everybody knows that."

"Sure," said Creighton. "And just how many tractors and combines did you see for sale on the streets? That's what TASA sends to Latin America—agricultural equipment. Not this dried milk and vitamin pill stuff you saw!"

Karen was not easily shaken. "What about spare parts? And fuel? And God knows what else?"

Creighton sounded as if he regretted beginning the exchange. "Sure, we send spare parts for tractors. But, my God, how many tractors do you think there are in the country? I'll tell you. There are practically none, except for what TASA's sent. Believe me, there is not a roaring black * market for spares!"

"That's what you say!"

Doug Travers scowled at Karen. Howard Creighton

merely shrugged. "Look," he told the room at large, "this is getting us nowhere."

Dr. Olivera did not agree. "What Mrs. Jenks says is true. She has seen things with her own eyes!"

The deliberate malice in his voice made Creighton redden with anger. But before he could speak, Carl Zimmerman's secretary appeared with another latecomer.

Señora Montoya was smiling brilliantly.

Chapter 12

Señora Montoya's electric presence had its usual effect. Quentin Fels overflowed with deference, rushing to set a chair for her. Manuel Olivera instantly grew cautious and reserved. Carl Zimmerman donned his full State Department manner. Creighton, Ben Safford and Doug Travers withdrew slightly from the limelight.

Only one person remained untouched. Karen Jenks waited impatiently for the bustle to subside before returning to Olivera's last words.

"You don't have to be an eyewitness to know that something fishy is going on at TASA! Not when you have people thrown out the twelfth floor! Why are you all too chicken to face up to the truth? I'll say it for you—here, or anywhere else. Barnes caught someone siphoning off the cream, and he got murdered because he was going to talk!"

She flung this accusation at them with burning intensity, as if expecting to be assaulted on the spot. The reaction, when it came, baffled her. Her ringing sentences triggered only a series of sparring matches, that led further and further from the main issue.

"Mr. Zimmerman," said Manuel Olivera with morose detachment, "I hope you will note that Mrs. Jenks has gone far beyond the scope of my statement."

"You don't have to remind me, Dr. Olivera," Carl Zimmerman replied. "And we're not keeping a record of this meeting."

"I hope to God not!" Howard Creighton thundered. "If I'm supposed to sit here and listen to some crazy kid calling me a thief—"

Señora Montoya raised her remarkable voice only slightly, but she dominated the room.

"That, of course, is nonsense, Mr. Creighton," she said with liquid assurance. "We all know Mrs. Jenks means well, even if her exaggerations are unfortunate. That is the prerogative of youth."

Karen Jenks was not grateful.

The señora proceeded: "But, of course, I must say, Mr. Zimmerman, that it is most improper for my colleague, Dr. Olivera, and me to associate ourselves with an inquiry concerning a purely American problem."

This gave Karen her chance.

"You're jumping to conclusions," she said coldly. "Who said it's an American problem? It seems to me there's plenty of room for siphoning, on the Nuevadorian end."

Score one for Karen, thought Ben Safford. There was no longer any patronizing indulgence on Señora Montoya's face.

Manuel Olivera, on the other hand, was amused. "But this is very interesting, Mrs. Jenks. There are more possibilities here than one would think. Perhaps I have been too narrow-minded. We must avoid that mistake in the future. People are greedy for things other than money . . ."

Dr. Olivera might have continued in this sibylline vein, but Howard Creighton had had enough. Placing muscular hands on the table, he half rose.

"Look, the purpose of this meeting seems to be a full-scale attack on TASA shipments. And I'm not going along . . ."

Señora Montoya made a light, restraining gesture. "Not a full-scale attack, Mr. Creighton. But, surely, an investigation, undertaken with care and discretion, would be welcome to all friends of both Nuevador and the United States. Can anyone deny that? I know you must agree, Mr. Creighton."

Howard Creighton glared angrily around the room. He was getting no support, Ben saw. Was that why he suddenly sounded so deflated?

"Oh, hell," he said with a shame-faced grin as he sank back into his chair. "OK, OK, I'll cooperate . . ."

The fireworks were over. The meeting was not. It went on for another hour without producing anything of interest to Ben. But he was still thinking.

"Doug," he said when chairs were being pushed back, "get Karen out of here. And do your best to keep an eye on her, for the time being."

Safford had no time to explain this request. Nor was he certain that he could account for a sudden uneasiness. Karen Jenks was in the clear when it came to the attack on Mrs. Barnes. But Ben was not sure that she was in the clear elsewhere.

Looking serious, Travers rose and moved around the table. Ben watched him lean over to speak in Karen's ear. He did not relax until Doug escorted her firmly from the room.

Diplomats might be able to forget murder. Ben Safford could not.

And Karen Jenks, with her fusillade of accusations, might be firing dangerously close to someone who had already murdered once.

"I'll take you home," Doug said flatly.

Karen wavered only a moment, then, almost indifferently, she replied, "OK."

Doug was relieved. Like Congressman Safford, he wanted to keep Karen as far from the action as possible. The question was, how to do it? Until now, good intentions had not been much help. But Karen's response to a simple, firm command was noted and filed.

They marched through the crowded lobby of the New State Building in silence. If it was not companionable, it was at least an armed truce. Doug examined his companion. She was deep in thought. Doug knew that meant trouble.

"Face it when it comes," he said to himself, unconsciously falling back on army lessons.

They reached the corner of 21st and C Streets at the height of the rush hour.

"We catch the bus over on Constitution Avenue," said Karen, rousing herself from her reverie.

"We take a taxi," Doug corrected her.

Again, that passive acceptance of higher authority. But this time, there was a gleam of mischief in Karen's expressive eyes.

Twenty minutes later, after a good deal of futile arm waving and whistling, they approached the crowd on Constitution Avenue, waiting for the R 8 bus.

"Sorry," said Doug shortly.

Karen turned to him. "What?" Clearly she had more important things to think about than taxis.

This self-possession suddenly stung Doug. "What was your husband like?" he startled himself by asking.

Karen thought a moment. "Jerry?" she said, as if looking back a long way. "We lived together for a year and a half, and I still don't know what he's like. We couldn't talk to each other. He wasn't interested in what I did—and I wasn't interested in what he did. Every single thing I care about bores him. Either there was nothing there to know—or I never hit the right key."

Doug was wondering how to reply when her face lit up and she laughed aloud. "But, you know, it was just as bad for him as it was for me. If you asked him what *I* was like, he'd probably say he never found the right key, either."

"You've lost me," Doug said, matching her honesty. "I don't understand that at all."

She looked up at him. "Nobody ever does—unless they've been through it."

Doug suddenly realized that he was not Karen's only listener. Behind them, a group of secretaries hung on every word. Fortunately, the bus finally arrived. Clambering aboard, they stood silent on the long swaying ride toward Capitol Hill.

Fifteen minutes later, they were walking down a twilit street, passing houses cascading sound. Ahead of them and behind them, were young people hurrying home from work. The men wore coats and ties, and carried evening papers under their arms; the girls wore trim cotton dresses and pumps, and carried bundles marked Woodward & Lothrop. But already the rackety doorways were disgorging identical young people in the uniforms of freedom—sandals, shorts, turtlenecks and barbaric medallions.

They reached 112 C Street and Doug followed Karen up the steps, almost colliding with a couple hurrying out.

"Hi!" they said to the world at large.

"Hi!" Karen replied.

"Say, Karen," said one of them looking incuriously at Doug, "Russ has been looking all over for you."

Karen had already gone ahead into the hallway and was looking over the pile of mail on the table. She gave no sign of having heard the last remark. But Doug was reminded that he had instructions to keep her out of trouble. Russ Gallagher certainly came under that heading.

"How about dinner?" he asked.

She paused, one hand on the banister. When she did speak, it was with unusual thoughtfulness. "Dinner? Why . . . why, yes. I'd like that."

She sounded, Doug thought, as if she had made an

important decision—and it wasn't about joining him for dinner. Was it something to do with Gallagher? Was Karen declaring her independence? He could try to find out over dinner.

"I'll be back to pick you up in the car," he said.

"Fine," she said, starting up the stairs. "Better make it an hour."

Somewhere in the back of the house, a telephone began ringing. Doug, who had turned to leave, was tempted to wait. Instead he continued outside; he would just have to hope that Russ Gallagher did not materialize during this particular hour.

There was no sign of him when Doug and his battered VW returned to C Street. But Karen Jenks was waiting on the sidewalk. As he pulled up, she swiftly let herself into the car with leggy grace.

"You look nice tonight," said Doug.

It was true; a perfectly simple black dress and a chain of lovely opals set off the sheen of blond hair. Karen might be a nuisance and a responsibility, but Doug had seen homelier ones.

They had not driven a block before he realized that there was something on her mind. He did not discover what until the waiter at Harvey's disappeared with their order.

"Look," Karen said rather hopelessly, "you're not going to like this."

Here was another departure, Doug thought. Karen Jenks was not in the habit of worrying about what people liked.

"After you dropped me off, I got a phone call. It was Manuel Olivera—" She broke off to see how he was taking it.

Doug was not going to let her see that this surprised him, that he had been expecting something about Russ Gallagher.

"He wants to talk to me about something," she went on.

"You've talked to him before," he reminded her.

Karen was too intent to respond to his mild jibe. "This is different. He wants to see me right away. He says it's urgent."

Doug waited in silence.

"He wants me to come over there tonight. And I said I would."

"Great!" said Doug.

She looked at him uncertainly, then picked her words with care. "I said that you'd come too. That we'd both be at his apartment at ten o'clock."

More than one question leaped to Doug's mind. He concentrated on the most important. "What did Olivera say to that?"

She sounded ingenuous. "He said that would be even better."

She was watching him anxiously.

He hesitated a moment before he said, "Well then, we can't disappoint him. We must be the first Americans Olivera has ever really wanted to see."

He thought she sighed with relief, but the arrival of the Shrimp Norfolk interrupted the conversation and left him free to try to figure things out. Dr. Olivera had been talking pretty big this afternoon. Could he be trying to pull a fast one on Karen? If he was, this enthusiasm for one of Congressman Ben Safford's aides was suspicious.

But Karen had been at the meeting, too. And sitting next to Olivera, Doug suddenly remembered. Could the two of them be cooking up something?

Suddenly, he put down his fork. If Karen Jenks was anybody's decoy, it was likely to be Russ Gallagher's.

"Karen," he said, "did Gallagher manage to get hold of you this evening?"

"He left a message," she said evasively.

"Did you call back?"

"I haven't had much time today," she said. Meeting his

116

steady gaze, she blushed slightly and added, "Oh, all right! I'm avoiding Russ."

"Oh?" said Doug. "Oh, here's the dessert menu—"

"Don't be so superior," she said heatedly.

He grinned. "Touché!"

Placated, she went on: "Russ has his faults, and I've always known it. I never thought they were any of my business. But today I realized that you can expect to disagree with people about a lot of things—but not about a poor woman who's been knocked over the head, and sent to the hospital." She raised her chin a fraction. "I simply decided that Russ isn't my kind of person."

This was as much of a concession as you would get from Karen, Doug decided. He hoped it was genuine. Certainly she sounded sincere enough. But with Manuel Olivera still waiting in the wings, Doug could not afford to be totally disarmed.

In fact, he would do well to consult Congressman Safford, he decided, asking for change for the phone. He could report these developments—and he might get some useful advice. But Safford was out. There was nothing further to do. Doug joined Karen and together they strolled out into the night.

Springtime is the loveliest time of the year in Washington, the one moment when the dogwood and cherry rival the marble and monuments. After sunset, the whole city glows with a soft tropical languor.

Doug and Karen strolled along Connecticut Avenue toward his car.

"Where does Olivera live?" he asked, holding the door.

"Near Dupont Circle," Karen replied.

Within minutes they were searching for a parking place. They located one a block from the neutral crackerbox where Olivera lived.

This time there was no velvet magic in the evening.

117

"Let's go," said Doug heartily. "And let me tell you, I expect the worst!"

"That's not a very helpful attitude," she retorted, crisply taking the lead.

Yet all this determination foundered. There was no reply to the buzzer.

After ringing for several minutes Karen turned to Doug at a loss.

"But he said . . ."

Just then a party of merrymakers, clearly leaving a cocktail party, came straggling through the main apartment door.

"Come on," Doug directed, swiftly keeping the door from closing. "With these apartments, these damned buzzers don't work half the time."

But up on the fourth floor, a vigorous tattoo on the knocker elicited no response.

Karen bent over to put her ear to the door.

"I think I hear a radio," she reported.

Losing patience, Doug grasped the knob and turned hard. The safety catch was not on. At once, the door swung open. Doug was almost propelled into Manuel Olivera's apartment. Karen hesitated, then followed him in.

It was the usual characterless room, with low ceilings and modern furniture. The phonograph, however, was still playing—with Lily Kraus delicately following the fine tracery of Mozart. On a glass-topped table between two chairs, a large ashtray held two cigars, their pungent aroma still suffusing the room. A spotlight near the sofa illuminated a large, unframed painting. The rest of the room was almost as dark as the outdoors.

But not quite.

"What the hell—?"

For a moment, Doug was immobilized as he stared down at the deeper shadow near his feet. "Karen, turn on that light!"

But the harsh brilliance of the overhead light was not necessary. Blinking slightly, Doug Travers squatted down on his heels.

And looked at his own right hand, red with blood.

And looked also at the body of Manuel Olivera.

Manuel Olivera was dead.

Chapter 13

Slowly Doug straightened. Olivera lay sprawled, face down, near one of the chairs. Blood from his smashed skull had poured over his collar and shoulders, to form a pool on the rug. It was already beginning to congeal around a heavy, primitive figurine.

That sandstone, Doug thought, won't hold a fingerprint.

Because it was clear enough what had happened. Two cigars, two indented pillows, two people talking. There were no signs of struggle. Had Olivera risen to usher his visitor out, when he was savagely struck down from the rear?

It was too late for a doctor, Doug Travers knew. But not for the police.

"Doug, let's get out of here!"

He turned to look at Karen. She was a foot behind him, silhouetted in the doorway.

"Come on," she whispered frantically. "No one will know we've been here!"

He ignored her words. "Give me a handkerchief, will you?" he asked without emotion.

Blindly she stared at him, then down at his crimson

hands. Still staring, she rummaged through her purse, found some tissues, and thrust them at him.

Doug kept his voice level. "You'd better shut that door."

She whirled to push it closed, then stood, backed against it. Her eyes were enormous. All color had drained from her face. Horrifyingly, she might have been an old woman.

Death can do this, Doug remembered, even to men in battle.

"We can't go, Karen," he explained. "We have to call the police."

"No!"

He stepped a pace forward. "Look, we'll wait outside. You don't have to look at him. I know it's not easy."

"Oh, my God!" It was a haunted cry.

Doug put out a comforting hand, but she recoiled.

"He's dead! Can't you see that? There's nothing we can do. Oh, God, why did we have to find him like this?" she burst out feverishly. "It will be questions and suspicion all over again. I can't stand any more!"

Her voice rose.

"We're calling the police," Doug interjected grimly.

She took a deep breath. "I won't! I won't!" She turned and fumbled at the doorknob.

He was at her side, and his hand on her shoulder was not gentle. "You're staying, Karen," he said flatly. "You have to."

"Damn you," she said in a half sob. "Damn you!"

"Sit down over there." He pushed her toward a chair in the far corner of the room, away from the body. No use trying to explain to Karen that leaving would only make things worse. He stood over her.

"Karen," he said, "what if Olivera told someone you were coming up here tonight? Think about it, won't you?"

She passed a trembling hand across her eyes, but did not answer.

He scowled at her for a moment, but only a moment.

Things had to be done. But as he dialed the police, he looked back at the bereft figure. Karen sat very still.

Nor had she said one more word when Captain Rigsby and his men arrived to turn Manuel Olivera's dull, characterless apartment into a nightmare laboratory.

"Then what?" Ben Safford prompted.

Travers rubbed a stubbled jaw. "Then the police got there. Photographers, fingerprinters—the whole works. Captain Rigsby sent us down to headquarters—for a real workout!"

"Exactly what does that mean?" Ben asked. "What kind of questions?"

Travers tried to recall the long session.

"They put a lot of effort into that hour before dinner when Karen was at C Street," he said, closing his eyes.

Ben nodded. "That's reasonable. But no one can claim that she could have gotten to Dupont Circle and back in an hour not with time out for murder."

"I know that," Doug said heavily, "but Karen . . ."

He shrugged, then continued, reviewing the endless questions about the State Department meeting, about Manuel Olivera's behavior, finally about the reason Olivera wanted to speak with Karen. He could still hear her bewildered cries.

"I don't know, I don't know!"

"They let us go about an hour ago," he concluded dully. "I took Karen home, then I figured you'd better know about this, so I came over."

There was no apology, although it was five o'clock in the morning.

He studied his shoes. Without looking up, he added, "I'm resigning, of course."

"Good boy," said Ben, to himself. Doug Travers was exhausted, but he was still functioning. Administrative assistants who find bodies and are questioned by the police are liabilities to their congressmen. Ben did not like to think of the headlines to come. Aloud he said, "OK. You've resigned, and I don't accept it. Now, think about work. We've got a lot to do."

Ben did not wait for Doug's thanks, but went on. "How is Karen?"

The guarded, constrained reply told him more than Travers intended.

"Janet's always telling me I don't understand women," said Ben. "She's right. I don't. But I do understand one thing. Karen Jenks has been through a lot, in the last few months. And she can take just so much."

Travers said nothing.

Ben rose, as an unexpected yawn caught him. He was suddenly conscious of the disadvantages of bathrobe and slippers, of the dusty light of first dawn.

"Well, this is no time for amateur psychology," he said. "Doug, you go home and try to catch some sleep. Be at the office by, say, ten o'clock."

"What are you going to do?"

Ben suppressed another yawn. "I'm going to try to take the sting out of this publicity. Which means, that I'm going to call Madge."

At just about the time that Congressman Safford was rousing his office staff and alerting them for the mess to come, other parts of official Washington were getting into action long before normal working hours. For if the murder of Manuel Olivera was a personal crisis for Karen Jenks, and a political pitfall to Ben Safford, it was more to local authorities.

"We've got to be very careful," said the pale little man to Captain Rigsby.

Rigsby simply looked at him. The pale little man was, like Rigsby, a member of the Washington Police Department, but he was not a policeman. Officially, he was Liaison

Officer with the Executive Branch; actually, he was assigned to cope with the diplomatic colony. Most of his work dealt with traffic offenses and parking violations.

"Haven't had a murder yet," said the pale man, whose name was Loomis. "But the drill should be the same. The State Department and the Nuevadorian Embassy—"

"Are going to be goddam tricky," Rigsby finished for him. It was still only six in the morning; they sat in Manuel Olivera's apartment, now dusty and derelict. Olivera's body was gone. The newspapers had been given only the baldest of facts; Rigsby's subordinates already had their orders.

Loomis ruminatively chewed his lower lip. "You know how the diplomatic corps reacts to traffic tickets?"

Rigsby, and every other member of the Washington Police Force, did.

"We'll be careful, Loomis," he said. "But we can only be so careful. If we can't question these people, we won't get anywhere. For crissake, it's perfectly possible that whoever killed Olivera is a member of the State Department, or the Nuevadorian Embassy."

"Let's hope not," said Loomis fervently. He looked bleakly into a tangle of official protests, squabbles about immunity and international law. "Still, we'll have to face that when we come to it. But will you try to keep things as calm as you can?"

Disgruntled, Rigsby looked around the apartment. "I'll do what I can," he said. "But the way things are developing —well, I can't guarantee anything."

Already, wheels were turning. First, there was the massive detail of standard operating procedure. Uniformed men had already fanned through the apartment house to ask Manuel Olivera's neighbors what they had seen, what they had heard, what they knew or guessed. Preliminary returns were already trickling in. No one knew Manuel Olivera. At the

124

moment, it was being claimed that no one had ever noticed Manuel Olivera. Nothing had been seen or heard.

Captain Rigsby knew that daylight would jog civic responsibility. An encounter in the elevator would come to light, or a borrowed tray of ice cubes. But he was not optimistic. Washington apartments are the homes of people who have hopes, dreams and interests elsewhere. Already, technicians had reported that Manuel Olivera's home was remarkably free of personal items: a few papers in the desk, very little food in the kitchen, a modest wardrobe in the closet. Apart from this, the apartment might still belong to the people from whom Manuel Olivera sublet it.

So, phase two of police inquiries was being implemented. Washington taxi drivers were being circularized, together with chance passersby and waitresses at the nearest restaurants. Similarly, back at headquarters, a very competent policeman was double-checking Manuel Olivera's diplomatic status, his driver's license, his known activities and movements. Certain files of the FBI were being consulted for information about political affiliations and contacts. Newspapermen to whom Olivera had given interviews were wakened. It was still early but the police already had a pile of data without much form.

A good many of the preliminaries came in the shape of lists. Across the room from Rigsby, two police specialists were translating and transcribing every word of Manuel Olivera's few papers.

". . . three borers, four drills. The next item on the list is one International Harvester tractor, Model 643, with rotary harrow attachment," one of them read aloud. "That makes fifteen items. The list is dated March 14, 1968 and the destination is Estancia Flora . . ."

Downtown, the list was coming via telephone. ". . . graduated University of Nuevador in 1948. Member, Students Democratic Social Progress Movement, Socialist Party, Nuevadorian Liberation Front . . ."

Even Barry Loomis was contributing. "Here's the list of Olivera's official trips in the U.S. since last June," he reported, not long after he had left Rigsby. "One speech at the University of Texas. Official observer, UN Conference on Fertilizers—got that?—"

Captain Rigsby was prepared to do a lot of sifting, but he had other irons in the fire. Manuel Olivera might have been a ranking official of the Nuevadorian Embassy, but he was also a man who had been present at the Sears Building when Phil Barnes was pushed to his death. Manuel Olivera had been an acting diplomat—but he had also been deeply embroiled in the accusations of Karen Jenks, in the rankling dispute between TASA and Nuevador, in the schisms and strains in the Nuevadorian Embassy.

So, as a precaution, Captain Rigsby was going to move swiftly to find out exactly what the other members of that particular controversy had been doing. Between five-thirty and ten o'clock, last night.

"That telephone call," a subordinate objected when Rigsby said as much. "Olivera called the Jenks girl at six-thirty."

"That's what she says," said Rigsby.

"But look, Captain, why should she lie—then turn up with this Travers guy to find the body? That doesn't make sense."

"Sense!" Rigsby snorted. "Nothing the Jenks girl does makes much sense to me." Since he was a fair man, he added, "That goes for the rest of them too. But, by Jesus, this time, I'm going to make some sense out of things."

Ben Safford was scooped up in this police activity by the time he reached Capitol Hill at eight o'clock.

Madge Anderson was in the office before him.

So, too, was a handsome young man in a well-cut Palm

Beach suit. He identified himself as Detective Wyatt and requested Congressman Safford's cooperation.

"My God, you don't think I killed Olivera, do you?"

Detective Wyatt and Madge both frowned at this statement. Probably neither of them had been up since five, Ben reflected. At any rate, Wyatt responded with something about routine.

But there was nothing routine about Detective Wyatt's subsequent interview with Safford. After establishing Ben's presence the previous evening at a banquet of the National Firefighters' Association, Wyatt moved on to the State Department meeting, Karen Jenks, Douglas Travers, and other subjects that Ben liked less and less.

"Whew!" he said, half-amused and half-irritated as he and Madge acknowledged Detective Wyatt's farewells. "He'll be more than a match for Señora Montoya."

But Señora Montoya was not next on Detective Wyatt's agenda. Quentin Fels was.

Fels was at the breakfast table when Detective Wyatt arrived.

"Olivera killed? Good heavens!" Fels sputtered. "What on earth . . . what? What was *I* doing last night? You don't mean to suggest . . ."

It took Detective Wyatt considerable time to extract a coherent account from Fels. But Fels finally admitted that he had hurried home to his bachelor quarters in Georgetown, changed into evening attire, then proceeded to a dinner appointment.

"At the White House. No doubt, you know that the President is entertaining the Prime Minister of Iceland. The Sears Iceland Project . . ."

Detective Wyatt took a dislike to this self-importance. Without sarcasm, he agreed it was unlikely that the murderer had slipped away from 1600 Pennsylvania Avenue and struck down Manuel Olivera before returning to the dinner party. Wyatt then pointed out that dinner at the

White House was late enough to leave a lot of Mr. Fels' time unaccounted for. Mr. Fels had no corroboration for his earlier movements, did he?

Fels was apoplectic. "Look here, I have absolutely no connection . . ."

Woodenly, Wyatt differed. "You're connected with this quarrel about the Jenks girl and the Nuevadorians. You sent her down there. This Barnes guy from TASA was killed in the Sears Building. Your connections are pretty good, Mr. Fels."

He left behind him a badly rattled man.

Wyatt caught up with Howard Creighton just as he was pulling into a reserved parking space outside the TASA building. His look of strain might have been the natural result of the morning rush hour. But, it developed, he had heard the bad news.

"Already?" he said wearily as Wyatt introduced himself. "Oh, yes. Somebody from the Nuevadorian Embassy called to tell me Olivera had been killed. It was on the morning news, too. God, when is this mess ever going to end?"

Wyatt duly noted that Howard Creighton accepted his own involvement in the search for Manuel Olivera's murderer without protest.

"God knows what's going on," Creighton said with suppressed violence. "Me? Hell, I went to that State Department meeting. Then I drove home. I didn't get home until —oh about eight-thirty. You can check with my wife. I went back to my office first. Then there was one helluva tie-up on the bridge. Not much of an alibi, huh?"

Wyatt did not comment, although he knew that Creighton's wife was already due for questioning.

Creighton took a deep breath, unconsciously bracing as they entered the TASA building. "Olivera was gunning for me and TASA," he said. "Everybody'll tell you that. I suppose you already know about that meeting yesterday? Well, I want to go on record. Olivera was gunning for

128

all Americans. We happened to be in his line of fire! It was just coincidence—because Phil Barnes got killed."

"You think there's a connection?" Wyatt asked.

Creighton smiled sourly. "The way things have been going, I'd be pretty naïve to hope that there's a jealous husband or a thief in the woodwork."

Again, Detective Wyatt refrained from comment.

Some of his colleagues were being even more watchful. In the gilt and crimson splendor of the Nuevadorian Embassy, Detectives Sparrow and Wilson were following very explicit instructions. They were avoiding direct questions. They were emphasizing cooperation and, of course, listening hard. The Ambassador, an aged dandy, had weighed official requests for a full two hours, then graciously agreed to extend his cooperation. Now he, a younger aide and Señora Montoya were, in effect, holding court for the police. Detectives Sparrow and Wilson had been greeted with flawless courtesy, and a strong atmosphere of favor conferred.

Also present were representatives of the State Department. Despite Barry Loomis' pleas, the Department had decided that in view of the prevailing tension and the extreme delicacy of U.S.-Nuevadorian relations, it was necessary to send diplomats in with the police. Carl Zimmerman, dressed more meticulously than usual, sat beside the Ambassador. Behind him, was a young assistant.

It was, Detective Sparrow thought to himself, one helluva way to conduct a police investigation.

"These are violent times and, as the world knows, Americans are a violent people," said Ambassador Zoluago. "Of a certainty, some madman has struck down Olivera. Already, I have asked my colleagues of the diplomatic corps to strongly press the United States Government for greater police protection."

Detective Sparrow nodded sympathetically. Carl Zimmerman went further. "The Secretary himself has been giving serious thought to increased precautions for members of the diplomatic corps, Your Excellency," he said.

"It is necessary," said His Excellency.

"Also, Excellency," murmured the aide, "prompt punishment of the author of this outrage."

Sparrow and Wilson remained deferential, although they knew they had hit a critical point. So far, the Nuevadorian Embassy had been remarkably slow to demand justice. There had been formal statements, but no insistence that authorities apprehend the murderer of Dr. Olivera.

And that had been a point of considerable interest to Captain Rigsby.

Señora Montoya stirred slightly. "Of course, we of the embassy wish to cooperate," she said with a half smile at the Ambassador, who nodded. "But serious problems exist. You must understand our position. Dr. Olivera was a Nuevadorian, a member of this embassy staff. The government of Nuevador must be assured that there are no political implications . . ."

Sparrow, picking his way carefully, thought he saw an opening. Softly, he asked, "Do you have any reason to suspect a political motive for the murder, Señora Montoya?"

Señora Montoya was annoyed. It was not clear whether the annoyance was directed at herself or at Detective Sparrow. Whatever she was going to say, was forestalled.

"It is well-known that Dr. Olivera was uncovering evidence of American interference in domestic Nuevadorian affairs," the young aide began with ill-concealed truculence. Before he could continue, Señora Montoya intervened:

"No, no," she said. "You are putting it too strongly, Rafael."

Her voice was almost maternal, but Rafael flushed hotly and subsided.

Señora Montoya exchanged a brief look with the Ambassador.

"We do not wish to convey the wrong impression," he said vaguely.

Señora Montoya was grave. "Dr. Olivera was an enthusiast. As you know, enthusiasm is often misleading."

The detectives tried to look as if this were profoundly wise. They did not altogether succeed, and for the first time Carl Zimmerman spoke. "Perhaps I can help on this point. Dr. Olivera was making investigations, as part of his job. There is no evidence of American misdeeds in Nuevador, nor of interference in internal Nuevadorian politics. In addition, there is no evidence of anything wrong in TASA shipments. And of course, we do not expect to find any such evidence. Yet at the same time, Dr. Olivera's watchfulness was very proper."

That wasn't much better, Sparrow thought to himself, but it pleased Señora Montoya. "Yes," she said. "That is very well put, Mr. Zimmerman."

There was an awkward silence. Both Sparrow and Wilson had been thoroughly briefed on Olivera's suspicions of both Señora Montoya, and the whole TASA program. They knew also about the factions in the Nuevadorian Embassy. Yet they were specifically prohibited from pursuing these points. Oddly enough, their silence elicited more comment than questions might have.

"No, there can be no reason to seek a political motive," said Señora Montoya, fully recovering her normal assurance. "It is only because Dr. Olivera was so zealous in his work, that his work leaps to mind. But my remark—as I see now—was most foolish. No doubt it was some criminal, intent upon robbery who struck him down."

"That may be so," Detective Sparrow said politely, "and we are making every effort possible along those lines. On the other hand, there is also the possibility of something in Dr. Olivera's personal life . . ."

He left the sentence unfinished.

Señora Montoya's eyebrows had risen.

Doggedly, Sparrow continued, despite a cautionary look from Carl Zimmerman.

"Can you tell me anything about Dr. Olivera's personal life?"

"But, no," said Señora Montoya, almost surprised, "I did not know Dr. Olivera socially." She made it sound like an utter absurdity. The Ambassador, Sparrow noted, hid a smile behind his frail old hand.

Detective Wilson was studying a notebook. "Just one further point. I believe you entertained at the embassy last night. We're having a hard time tracing Dr. Olivera's movements. Now, am I correct in saying that Dr. Olivera did not attend this party?"

Again, Carl Zimmerman stirred. Under no circumstances, the instructions ran, were Sparrow and Wilson to ask for alibis.

Señora Montoya was looking steadily at him.

No fool, this one, Wilson thought. She was daring him to go one step further.

Detective Wilson looked back with pellucid innocence. He saw an uncontrollable flicker of satisfaction, before he let his own eyes drop. Wilson was used to diplomats, but Señora Montoya, he decided, was too foreign for him.

But she hadn't killed Olivera. Four employees of the Acme Catering Service were emphatic on that point. Señora Montoya had been a gracious hostess from cocktails until the embassy party broke up at eleven.

"Thank you for your cooperation," said Detective Sparrow gratefully.

Carl Zimmerman's sigh of relief was almost audible.

Many hours later, impressions were being exchanged.

"No," said Señora Montoya to the phone, "I am a good friend of the Americans, as you know. But I think frankly, we shall never know what happened. It is my opinion that the police have no idea of what to do. What? Oh, I do not think there will be serious repercussions, as you put it . . . Let me be frank, U.S.-Nuevadorian relations are undergoing a difficult stage but, once the TASA shipments resume, I think time will resolve the problems . . . What? . . . Oh yes, that is essential. The TASA shipments must be resumed . . ."

Carl Zimmerman was also on the phone.

"Yes, of course I'm worried. This whole situation is . . . What? Well, what else can I think? First, Olivera comes up with these damn fool accusations, then he's murdered . . . What? Yes, the police did ask me, and I was home with my wife. Where the hell would I be at that hour? . . . No, I was not at the Nuevadorian Embassy . . ."

There were many phone calls that day and for many after.

Chapter 14

For two weeks, the police continued to dig—from Embassy Row to Garrett Park, Maryland. They did not hit pay dirt. Captain Rigsby cast his nets wider and wider, from Philip Barnes' church affiliation to Carl Zimmerman's habits. He learned about Karen Jenks' ex-husband, and about Quentin Fels' taste in literature. He learned that Howard Creighton was unhappily married, that Señora Montoya had a famous jewelry collection, that Russ Gallagher had spent the evening of the Olivera murder at a sit-in at George Washington University. There remained too many things he did not know. Who had murdered Olivera? Who had struck down Mrs. Barnes?

And why?

Ignoring public outrage, Rigsby hunched his bulky shoulders against the onslaught and doggedly went on rooting out facts, in the hope that one of them would tell him who—and why. However, if public outrage did not produce results from the police, it did start hares in the halls of Congress.

"Well now," Congressman Val Oakes mused, "who would

have thought our committee was supposed to be a watch-dog for TASA?"

His fellow committeemen were silent.

"Did you know that, Ben?" Oakes persisted.

Ben Safford grunted.

"Christ! None of us did," said Tony Martinelli, his dark eyes bright with interest. "We thought our job was just to cut foreign aid. But if these nutboys push through a TASA investigation, it's a cinch the whole mess'll be tossed into our laps."

Elsie Hollenbach cleared her throat in a ladylike manner.

"I do not think it advisable to become involved with TASA at this juncture. As we have not kept abreast of TASA's activities"—here she examined her colleagues with some censure—"we cannot be particularly useful."

"That's it, Elsie!" Martinelli said warmly, jumping at a way out. "Now's no time for us to get mixed up in this mess. So TASA's been playing games! We don't want to give anybody the idea that we've been playing with them."

Mrs. Hollenbach was not thrown off stride by this bluntness. "I think," she continued, "that the House should demand an investigation by the State Department."

Oakes, who had tilted his chair back and rested his feet in a drawer, sleepily nodded agreement. "Good for you, Elsie. That gets us off the hook. I didn't think you had it in you."

Mrs. Hollenbach compressed her lips. She had strong views about evading one's responsibilities. These views brought out the worst in Eugene Valingham Oakes. Their clashes on the subject were becoming legendary.

In fact, quite a lot about Elsie was becoming legendary, Ben Safford thought as he helped Tony soothe ruffled feathers. Ben remembered her arrival to fill out the term of her deceased husband. Eighteen months later, party regulars in California were surprised to find the Hollenbach machine stronger than ever. They began to realize that Elsie had been running the show for a long time. She was more than a vote getter; she was fast becoming a power in the House. The right committee appointments came her way. A chairmanship was in sight. Soon there was bound to be a Hollenbach Act. More to the point, Val Oakes recognized this. A year ago he had bought one genteel wine glass and enlarged his liquor supply.

So Mrs. Hollenbach was sipping sherry as she reluctantly agreed that now was no time to run around seizing initiatives.

"You're right, Val. We'll let the people over at State handle this."

But the State Department was way ahead of them. At five o'clock that afternoon, a press release from the White House disclosed that the matter was in the hands of the Government Accounting Office. Reaction was immediate.

"Jesus!" Tony Martinelli exclaimed. "They must mean business."

Some civil servants caught the news in a bar. "You heard what they did?" they asked a latecomer. "Those poor fish over in TASA."

Elsie Hollenbach was dictating answers to correspondence. "You may place every confidence in the probity of the Government Accounting Office," she said crisply. "I join with you in hoping for a speedy resolution of . . ."

In short those three initials meant that a decisive step had been taken. The ax, as Ben Safford knew, was about to fall.

Not many people outside of Washington have heard of the GAO. But everyone in Washington knows that it is famous for the painstaking thoroughness of its examination of financial records. The GAO is not called in unless the government wants to track down every single dollar and cent. The announcement that the GAO was looking into TASA aid to Nuevador, therefore, triggered almost as many conversations as the murder of Manuel Olivera.

Carl Zimmerman had joined Ben Safford for a drink after work.

"Thank God, the State Department had enough sense to keep clear of this," said Zimmerman, emerging from a long cold glass of beer. "But I feel sorry for the guys over in TASA. The whole place is being torn apart by the GAO, the current shipment to Nuevador is bogged down and, on top of everything else, Phil Barnes seems to have been their workhorse."

Safford nodded.

"Creighton himself told me that Barnes always took care of the details," he said.

"Everybody there says the same thing. Barnes was one of these fussy perfectionists. He checked deliveries himself, he made suppliers toe the line. When they were getting the monthly shipment to Nuevador ready, he'd have stuff sent over from the warehouses, and then he'd send it straight back if things weren't just right. The GAO boys told me that the warehouse crews hated him, but they'd be surprised if anybody managed to pull anything on him."

"One way or another we should know before long. The government accountants work pretty fast," Safford commented.

Zimmerman raised a finger to flag the waitress for more beer. "The whole thing is beyond me. You know, TASA handles billions of dollars' worth of aid. It's got really big programs in Brazil and Argentina and Chile. My God, you could lose a hundred thousand dollars' worth of stuff and it would barely be noticed. But the Nuevador operation is different. Our aid there is just a sop to public opinion. TASA sends out twelve big crates of machinery every month. The whole business is peanuts!"

137

"I hadn't realized it was that small," Ben observed.

"There's another thing." Zimmerman was exasperated. "This isn't like the vitamin pills and dried milk your friend Karen Jenks is always bleating about. If you pinch a couple of bottles of pills from a massive shipment, it takes a detailed inventory to find out something's missing. But if a tractor goes over the hill, you have to be blind to miss it."

Everything that Zimmerman said was true but, as Safford reminded him, it wasn't their problem.

"Except of course that it brings the Nuevadorians onto your doorstep," he conceded.

Zimmerman grinned. "The Nuevadorians are on a different warpath. You know, Rigsby went through all the papers in Olivera's apartment. And, guess what Olivera was up to?"

Safford said it could be almost anything.

"He'd gone to the Nuevadorian Customs Department," Zimmerman said. "He got the lowdown on every single thing the Montoyas bought in America and imported into Nuevador. They own the Estancia Flora—that's the biggest landholding in the country. Olivera was checking to see that they brought in exactly what they declared."

"And did they?" Ben asked him.

"Not only did they bring in what they declared, they paid every penny of customs. All Olivera proved was that the Montoya operation is legitimate," Zimmerman replied.

"Then why the warpath?" Ben asked.

"Señora Montoya," said Zimmerman, "is furious that anybody had the effrontery to meddle in her affairs. That seems to include Rigsby, too."

But, if Señora Montoya was furious, she did not let it show as she joined Quentin Fels. It was intermission time at a benefit night of the Washington Symphony for Peruvian earthquake victims.

"Is that Howard Creighton over there?" Fels asked. He

138

had led Señora Montoya to a banquette and was hovering nervously over her.

"Oh, I do not think so," she said, drawing her taffeta skirts aside to make room. A regal gesture invited Fels to be seated. "Mr. Creighton is too busy these days. This investigation at TASA continues day and night."

"And week after week!" Fels was bitter. "If you ask me, it's Gestapo tactics."

"You are too severe," she said mildly. "These little disruptions are to be expected from time to time."

This serenity ruffled Fels.

"Little disruption? Between Karen Jenks, the police, and the GAO, I'm afraid that everything we planned in Nuevador will be wrecked."

Señora Montoya became reassuring. "No," she said. "You must not be disheartened. Remember, instead, our talks in Montecigalpa, the valuable assistance you offered."

Fels was unconvinced. "I'm afraid . . . I'm afraid . . ."

Many people in Washington were afraid, as the days passed with Manuel Olivera's murder still unsolved, and the GAO findings still a subject for speculation. Wednesday morning resolved one of these tensions. The GAO submitted its report; TASA's aid program in Nuevador was absolutely aboveboard. This verdict surprised official Washington. Even more surprising was the amount of supporting evidence the GAO had found.

"Just listen to this list," Tony Martinelli urged. He read aloud:

"March 17, 1968 . . . four milking machines . . . two tractors with rotary harrows . . . five hundred feet of irrigation piping . . . fifteen drills with full set bits . . . one combine . . . three borers . . . spare parts for a binder . . ."

"So?" asked Val Oakes, looking bored.

"They've tracked down everything," Tony explained.

"Here's the present location of every single thing TASA shipped on March 17th. The tractors are on a farm in the valley now. The combine is being run by some cooperative. All those spare parts were for a binder in the dairy that's getting the milking machines."

Ben Safford was beginning to feel that he never wanted to hear the word Nuevador again. Moodily he helped himself to some of Val's bourbon.

"Well, after all, the GAO is supposed to track things down," he said.

"I tell you one thing, Ben," Oakes roused himself to say. "We were right to stay out of this. Things have come to a pretty pass when people expect a congressman to run around looking for old batteries."

"Oh, I don't think anybody expects us to do that."

Martinelli impatiently brushed aside these interruptions. "That's not what I mean, Val. They say they traced everything. Every single piece of cable."

"Just so long as it's them and not me."

"Now, I ask you, is that how any aid program operates?"

"What exactly do you mean, Tony?" Ben asked curiously.

"I mean it proves that there's something fishy about this program! TASA's too good to be true."

And Tony Martinelli flashed a wicked smile.

Chapter 15

Karen Jenks saw nothing to smile about.

"I don't know what good that was supposed to do!" she said, stalking away from her latest session with Captain Rigsby.

Doug looked down at her. There was no longer any sign of the white-faced girl who had been so badly shaken by Manuel Olivera's body two weeks ago. Of course, Doug thought, Karen was resting between police grillings, which at least put an end to her TV appearances. He, himself, was spending the intervals working full-time for Congressman Safford. He had been keeping his temper under control for two weeks. He did not intend to lose it now.

"Be grateful he's still letting us go," he told her. "Did you say you wanted a phone?"

"Yes, I promised my father I'd call."

Doug knew she was avoiding the house on C Street which was now split into violent pro-Gallagher and pro-Jenks factions.

"If it's long distance, why don't you call from my apartment?"

"Thank you." Karen was formal.

They drove to Doug's apartment in smoldering silence. Once there, Doug left Karen to dump her chunky shoulder bag on the couch and marched into the kitchenette. When he reappeared with Scotch and ice cubes, Karen's temper exploded.

"Thank you," she said, accepting the drink. "To be honest, I'm getting sick and tired of thanking you."

For, innate honesty had forced Karen to admit that Douglas Travers had saved her from an act of incredible folly. Left to her own devices, she would have made herself a prime murder suspect two weeks ago. Since then, he had supported her steadily at every police interview and never once raised the subject.

Now he knew what she meant.

"It's natural that you were upset that night," he said amiably. "Olivera wasn't a pretty spectacle."

"And natural that you remained cool, calm and collected, I suppose," she retorted.

"Well, I've seen a lot more bodies than you have."

This was unanswerable, but it stung Karen.

"I suppose you think that's something to be proud of. Two years as a murderer in Vietnam!"

But Douglas Travers had had this kind of conversation before.

"Yes. I got drafted while people like your husband were sitting out their deferments in Ivy League colleges!"

"You leave my husband out of this!"

"Why? Because he's making a life's work out of ducking things?"

"No." Karen stood up. "Because I don't want to talk about him, and it's none of your business."

"That's rich. Karen, you're not the girl to tell anybody to mind his own business."

Karen did not take up the challenge. He looked at her with amusement in his eyes. She announced stiffly that she was placing her call. After preliminaries with the operator, she waited for the call to go through.

With a final touch of hauteur she said: "By the way, I'm reversing the charges on this call."

"I never doubted it for a moment," Doug said blandly.

Karen was saved by a crackle from the phone. She turned swiftly to greet her father.

Doug let his head rest against the chair and idly eavesdropped. Karen's side of the conversation was sprinkled with exclamations. "For heaven's sake, Daddy, of course everything's all right . . . Well, I don't care what people in Newburg are saying . . . Oh, my God, why does Aunt Clara have to butt in?"

But the character of the call changed completely when Karen's father was succeeded by her mother.

"Eighteen months is all right, Mother . . . Dr. Spock says . . . No, I don't think it's a good idea to let go of the diaper service, yet . . . Yes, I know, but he's bound to show some signs of interest . . ."

Doug saw this was the other Karen, the one he knew nothing about. As soon as she put down the phone, he realized that his Karen had reappeared.

"I didn't like that crack about minding my own business," she said. "I'm not ashamed of being interested in other human beings. I don't believe in people building walls around themselves."

He laughed aloud. "You're kidding yourself. You don't have a clue about other people. Look at you and Russ Gallagher."

"What about me and Russ Gallagher?" Karen demanded.

"Were you finding out about him? Were you communicating with him? Anyone who wasn't blind could see that he didn't give a damn about your problems. Even that little kook, Maureen, could see it. He was using you, the same way you were trying to use him. Did you know anything about him? Did you care? Hell, no! Then we have

143

a big song and dance when someone blackjacks Mrs. Barnes. You're shocked at his reaction."

"I don't put people into neat little pigeonholes, the way you do. The trouble with you is that you sit behind your defenses, being superior. It's all right for you to use Maureen because you're so important, because it's part of your job." She was blazingly angry. "That's the most important thing in the world, isn't it? That rotten little job. It's all you care about. You don't care about people. They don't mean anything in your scheme of things—"

The control of two weeks suddenly snapped. Doug Travers was furious. "You listen to me! It's time you grew up. Who's been holding your hand for the last two weeks? Who's hauled you out of every mess you got yourself into? You've been barreling along, making trouble wherever you go. Has it ever occurred to you that TASA *is* people? Has it occurred to you that Ben Safford is a human being—not just your congressman? Sure, you're interested in people— until they become a problem. You ditch your husband. You dump your baby on your parents. You wash your hands of Russ Gallagher. Let me tell you, baby, being interested in people is great, and it doesn't cost you anything either! Why don't you try doing something for them, for a change? You'll find it comes a lot more expensive, but you might turn into an adult in the process."

He broke off suddenly, seeing that she was as pale as she had been on the night of Olivera's murder. His tirade had vented his anger. Now he was only weary. And he remembered that these last two weeks had been hard on Karen, too.

"Look, I'm sorry . . ." he began.

In a broken voice, she said: "Forget it!"

"No, I shouldn't have said that, but you touched me on the raw."

Her head went up.

"Sure, I touched you on the raw. I said you used Maureen. You don't like to think of yourself as using people."

"Why the hell drag Maureen into this?" he growled.

Karen showed a flash of spirit. "Why drag Russ Gallagher into this? Why drag my husband into this?"

Doug could feel his temper rising again. He spoke carefully. "Because they've got something to do with you. Maureen has nothing to do with me."

"Oh, stop acting like a lawyer!"

"Why the hell can't you be consistent?"

Karen shook her hair aside. It had become disheveled, so that the loose strands caught the light and turned it into a golden aureole around her head.

"What's so bloody wonderful about consistency?" she demanded. "Life isn't consistent, love isn't consistent, people aren't consistent, so I'm not consistent. Can't you get that through your thick head?"

"You could try," Doug said almost absently. He was staring at her, as if for the first time seeing the tossed hair, the flushed cheeks, the proud carriage of her head.

"Well, I'm not going to try! I don't want to try!" It was a wild protest.

Doug sounded far away. His words were uncritical, almost judicious.

"You're behaving like a child. You don't know what you want."

She thrust out her arms blindly.

"Go away!" she cried. "Go away. Will you get out of here?"

But the echoes of these passionate words had barely died away before Douglas Travers suddenly realized exactly what it was that he wanted.

"No," he said evenly, "I'm not going away. Far from it."

When he swept her to him, he could feel only angry resistance. Then her mouth opened under his.

Chapter 16

Ben Safford, also, was making long distance calls to Newburg, Ohio.

"After all, Ben," said his sister Janet, "this is an election year! And this Karen Jenks uproar is getting a lot of publicity."

Ben was annoyed. He did not have to be reminded that this was an election year. He pointed out that Karen Jenks was more Newburg's responsibility than his.

"That's it. She's a local girl," said Janet obscurely. "Then, too, these rumors about TASA aid to Nuevador—"

"Janet," Ben cut in, "an all-out effort has just accounted for every American dollar spent on technical assistance in Nuevador." He did not add that some people thought TASA's books were too tidy. Particularly after two murders which were still baffling the police. It was just as well that he had not introduced further complications since Janet was going straight to her own point:

"Ben, I think you'd better schedule a trip home."

For this, Ben had no answer.

146

As a result, forty-eight hours later he was pulling the car into the driveway at 8 Plainfield Road, having put behind him a long morning of work in Newburg.

Taking the turn too sharply, Ben grazed the gate post. His brother-in-law, Fred Lundgren, carefully put down the hose and strolled over to survey the damage. Ben had managed to dent the fender and to scrape the newly painted post. Moreover, the car belonged to the Lundgren Ford Agency ("Biggest Ford Dealer in Southern Ohio"). Fortunately, Fred had the good-humored imperturbability of the big man.

"But it beats me, Ben," he remarked, abandoning the garden for a drink on the porch, "why your driving never improves. God knows you've been at it for years."

They were in wicker chairs when Janet bumped open the screen door to join them with a tray.

"Be fair, Fred," she said. "Ben hasn't had a serious accident, oh, for three or four years."

Fred took charge of the pitcher. "You're forgetting that elm tree on Mrs. Schellmyer's lawn," he said, pouring carefully.

"That's right," said Janet seriously, "I am."

Ben grinned lazily at them. Justified jibes at his driving were part of home to him—as much as the sycamore trees in the front yard, the big old house, and Janet and Fred themselves.

"I'll have Bill touch up the fence," Fred remarked. "After you've gone, Ben. How did things go today?"

For a minute, Ben reviewed the morning's work.

"Well, as Val Oakes keeps saying, murder doesn't help win elections."

Both his relatives nodded tacit agreement, and Ben summarized the reports of his local lieutenants. As always, proximity to murder and to scandal, never did an incumbent any good. It let the opposition bear down heavily on its own closeness to local people, problems and virtue.

"Lew Frome is going to plug that theme hard," said Janet. "The PTA, the United Fund—all of that." She did not sound alarmed, being very capable along those lines herself.

"Then too," Ben went on philosophically, "Ed said that Lew is planning to capitalize on the fact that there isn't much local interest in Nuevador—or in aid programs."

Fred looked out at the lawn and gave his advice:

"That's true as far as it goes, Ben, but you can carry it too far. Now, Lew Frome is going to misplay this—because that's the kind of guy he is. He'll make a big pitch about foreign entanglements—and never realize that he's insulting the intelligence of Newburg. Times change. You'd be surprised how sophisticated some of these folks are getting."

"You mean Lew Frome would be," said Janet tartly.

Fred accepted the comment and went on: "Then too, you've got an ace in the hole. You're involved in all this because you're taking care of a home-town girl. That'll go down big with everyone."

Gloomily, Ben replied that he could not see Karen Jenks as a campaign asset. If the murders of Philip Barnes and Manuel Olivera were still hanging fire in November, any politician unlucky enough to have ever met them was going to be in trouble.

"And if those murders are solved," Ben went on grimly, "it's inevitably going to be someone I know. Probably someone I've been photographed with."

He fell silent, mentally running down a list of names: Carl Zimmerman, Quentin Fels, Señora Montoya, Howard Creighton—even, God forbid, Karen Jenks.

Janet interrupted this somber roll call by revealing that she had been doing her homework. "I think you're wrong about the Jenks girl, Ben," she said. "Unless, of course . . . well, let's just hope not. But look on the bright side. Assume that she's an innocent young girl, who's somehow gotten involved in two horrible murders."

148

"Even under the best of circumstances," Ben said frankly, "I don't think that's the way we can sell her. Not to anybody who's ever met her, that is."

Janet ignored him and continued, "I don't know her parents. The Kimballs have only been in town for three or four years. But he's an executive out at Harvester, they live over at Cloverdale Manor, and they're active in affairs out that way."

"Hmm," said Ben, brightening slightly. Cloverdale Manor was a new upper-income housing section, designed for the corporate executives attracted by the growing industries of Newburg County. Newburg was in the process of transition and Cloverdale Manor was pointing the way: already a good many farms of Ben's youth had disappeared, there was improved service from Newburg Airport, and Main Street now included several expensive specialty shops.

Politically speaking, Cloverdale Manor was up for grabs. Ben did not have to ask the next question.

"Last election," Janet reminded him, "you lost Wards Seven and Eight—which include Cloverdale and most of Lincolnwood by three thousand votes."

"And I expect," said Fred comfortably, "that they're all very interested in international aid programs, out that way."

Ben laughed. "You make it sound like a disease, Fred. You just don't like them because they buy Cadillacs instead of Fords."

Fred Lundgren could buy and sell most of Cloverdale. "I like them fine, Ben. They buy Lincolns, too, remember. And now and then a Thunderbird for the little woman. Listen, I saw them coming."

Businessman, clubwoman, and politician agreed that a visit from Congressman Benton Safford (D., Ohio) to Mr. and Mrs. Milo Kimball, parents of Karen Kimball Jenks, would be time well spent.

"Besides," said Janet, rising to begin dinner preparations,

"from what you've told me about the girl, I'm dying to know what the parents are like."

"You said it, I didn't," replied Ben.

Ben's first impression of the Kimballs was that they seemed too young to have a grown daughter. Let alone a grandson.

He had telephoned after dinner to find the Kimballs surprised but pleased at the prospect of a visit from their congressman. Then, to the accompaniment of parting cautions from Fred, he drove out four miles to Cloverdale Manor's entrance gates. There he immediately became lost in a bewildering spiral of roadways.

The Kimballs were rather pleased about this, too.

"People always get lost," said Mrs. Kimball when Ben apologized.

"That's right," said her husband. "I should get some of those little maps printed up. Come on in, Mr. Safford."

Ben entered a vaulted living room, where lime-green carpeting stretched from a fieldstone fireplace to ceiling-to-floor windows framing a patio and, beyond it, a swimming pool gleaming iridescently. It was all, Ben thought, a far cry from the Newburg he knew.

Mrs. Kimball was not so much an older version of her daughter as a variation. Her radiant blond hair was tossed into a short cap of curls; she was deeply tanned, with fine lines around Karen's startling blue eyes. She wore a crisp white shirt over sharkskin slacks. An ornately jeweled wrist watch matched the diamonds on her fingers.

"We're so grateful for all that you're doing for Karen," she said warmly.

But, as the conversation developed, the Kimballs seemed remarkably free from anxiety about their daughter. They were more concerned with Karen as young rebel than as murder suspect. Of course, Ben reminded himself, they were getting their information from Karen.

"Karen has always been very independent," said Mrs. Kimball over coffee. "Why, when she was fourteen years old, she spent the Teen-in-Europe Summer in Grenoble. She lived with a French family."

"Oh yes," said Ben.

Milo Kimball, also heavily tanned, drew on a large pipe that made him look more boyish than ever. "Of course, that's the only way to really know people, in a foreign country." He had a deep baritone voice.

Ben agreed, then said cautiously that Karen had certainly thrown herself into her Nuevadorian experience.

Mrs. Kimball said: "It helped her a lot to be able to speak the language."

Mr. Kimball nodded. "I've always said that that's the only way to get to know people. Speaking their language."

One thing Ben saw. He did not speak the Kimballs' language. He proceeded more cautiously.

"I understand that Karen has been coming home week ends," he said. "No doubt she's briefed you about recent developments."

Mrs. Kimball smiled her agreement, while her husband nodded.

"Karen comes home to see Jim, junior," she said. "Such a beautiful baby. And he already has a mind of his own."

Her husband, on the other hand, answered Ben directly. "You mean these murders, don't you? Karen says that all this publicity is sidetracking people from the real issues. That's why she's glad to have you helping her."

This observation floored Ben. It was one thing to be calm in the face of danger. It was another not to recognize that danger. Did Karen's parents understand her position? He began to think not.

Of course, *Look* and CBS had publicized Karen, the gadfly. It was the *Washington Post* that was headlining Olivera's murder. And Newburg was a long way from Washington.

151

He roused himself to find Mrs. Kimball speaking: "Of course, we told her she was too young to get married. But we've never laid down the law to any of our children . . ."

Her husband took up the theme.

". . . Karen has always been a top student. And very level-headed. But, when it turned out to be a mistake, we all agreed that divorce was the only right thing . . ."

"All?" Ben asked, surprised.

"Bill and Dorothy Jenks," Mrs. Kimball explained. "Jim's parents. Dorothy is a wonderful person. But we all agreed that having Karen and Jim stay together wouldn't be fair to them—or to little Jim either."

Ben wrenched the conversation away from divorce. He asked about the week end of the attack on Mrs. Barnes.

"Do you know the police have been here?" said Milo Kimball, frowning. "They seemed to want some sort of alibi for Karen. The most ridiculous thing I've ever heard. Not only did we tell them that Karen was here, we produced many neighbors who had seen her. And I don't mind telling you, I was pretty blunt with the chief. I told Briggs just how damn foolish the whole thing was. That's why I'm glad to have you looking after Karen's interests. Myself, I think she should come home. But of course, she can't leave her work."

Ben tried to bring Kimball out of the clouds by suggesting the Washington police might object to the departure of an important witness—if not suspect.

Kimball was not shaken. "I understand that point of view," he said reasonably. "And we've always emphasized to the children that they have duties as citizens of their communities. Just because they were fortunate enough to be raised in privileged circumstances doesn't mean that they can evade their responsibilities."

Ben decided it was time to leave.

"I just don't understand them at all," he reported early

next morning as Fred and Janet drove him to the airport. "If Ellen or Jan"—his nieces—"had gotten themselves into this kind of mess, you and Fred would have gone crazy."

From the backseat, Janet disagreed. "Things change, Ben, just as Fred said."

"Oh, come on, Janet!" he replied. "You know you and Fred kept eagle eyes on the boys. And as for the girls— well, if Ellen got married at eighteen, had a baby, got divorced, then started chasing around South America—"

"I'd tan her hide," said Fred ferociously. All of his children had made good, suitable marriages and were now spread from Ohio to California, doing exactly what Fred approved of.

"Not these days, you wouldn't," said Janet. "You'd probably do what this Mr. Kimball is doing. I tell you, things change—including how parents treat their children. Not to speak of what young people do."

Excellent driver though he was, Fred took his eyes from Route 18 long enough to shoot a look at his brother-in-law. And Ben agreed with the unspoken "Oh yeah?" At the same time, he suspected, there was something in what Janet was saying. There usually was.

Three hours later on that Sunday morning, he found himself back in Washington. According to the newspapers he had picked up at the airport, nothing new had broken. The police remained tight-lipped about "continuing" investigations and leads about the Olivera murder. Government sources were maintaining complete silence.

Nevertheless, Ben decided during the long taxi ride from Dulles Airport, it was too much to expect that his trip to Ohio had coincided with a three-day truce. Well, the one advantage of an administrative assistant high on the list of murder suspects was that he should know what the police—and others—were up to. Ben leaned forward and changed his directions to the driver.

Doug Travers, tying the belt of his bathrobe, answered the door. At sight of his visitor, he seemed to be dumfounded.

Puzzled, Ben said, "I'll just take a minute, Doug. If you can give me a fast rundown on what's been happening, I won't have to ask you to come into the office."

When Travers did not reply, Safford took a step into the living room and continued: "I'm particularly interested in whether the police—"

Then his eye fell on the coffee table. There, spilling its contents over the battered mahogany, was the all-too-familiar pouch of native leather with heavy silver initials.

K and J.

With an automatic reflex, Ben carefully did not look at the sofa, but kept talking:

"On second thought, I think we can take care of this at the office tomorrow morning."

By then, he was hurrying down the long hallway. Despite himself, he could not suppress a grin. No matter what Karen Kimball Jenks' father maintained, there was more than one way to get to know people.

Chapter 17

Fortunately, a social obligation took Ben out of his office the next day. It would be a good thing, he decided, if a little water went over the dam before he and Doug Travers encountered each other. But he could think of better ways to escape than attending Manuel Olivera's funeral.

"And anyway," he grumbled, "why bury him in Washington? Why not in Nuevador?"

At his side, Howard Creighton stirred. "As late as last week they were planning to fly the body home. There was going to be a big funeral in Montecigalpa. Then suddenly they changed their minds. If you ask me, they got cold feet. They were afraid of a riot. So they dug up something about Olivera wanting a simple funeral wherever he happened to die. And here we all are."

If this was Nuevador's idea of simplicity, Safford wondered what the full production would have been like. He and Creighton were at the graveside with the entire diplomatic corps, a large delegation from the State Department, and many other dignitaries. Manuel Olivera, as was to be expected, had been a free thinker. This had not kept his government from starting the day with high mass at Washington Cathedral. When the hushed mourners entered the church at midday, the thermometer had been hovering at the top of the seventies. Now, two hours later, both temperature and humidity were threatening to break into the nineties. The prevailing attire consisted of dark business suits, starched white shirts and black ties. Safford, cautiously easing his shirt collar from the back of his neck, suddenly remembered that many countries, when posting diplomats to Washington, give them tropical pay allowances.

"At least," he said, following his train of thought, "the Embassy will be air-conditioned." Still before them was a reception at the Nuevadorian Embassy.

"Hello, Congressman. This is some turnout they got for Olivera, isn't it?"

It took Ben a moment to identify the speaker. "Rigsby! I didn't recognize you at first. What are you doing here?"

Captain Rigsby smiled sourly. "It's a tradition in the department. We always send a man to the funeral. Of course, most murder victims don't get this kind of send-off."

Safford let his eyes rove over the crowded cemetery. "I shouldn't think this one would help you much. Everybody's here as part of his job."

The policeman nodded. "It's very different from Philip Barnes' funeral. That was just the family and his church friends and a few people from TASA."

"Barnes? Oh, of course." Ben had almost forgotten that murder. He admitted as much.

"We haven't forgotten," Rigsby said. "His family hasn't forgotten. I was talking to Mrs. Barnes just yesterday, when she came in for the car keys."

"Is Mrs. Barnes all right, now?" Ben asked.

"Yes. She went from the hospital to her sister's. That's why she didn't pick up the car before."

156

"What car?"

"Barnes' car. He parked it in a garage near the Sears Building the day he was murdered and the garage didn't notify us until days later. By that time Mrs. Barnes was in the hospital and we still had his keys, of course. But now that's all taken care of, and she's got the car back. And it's practically the only thing about that murder that has been cleared up, if you ask me."

Safford was not inclined to argue with this police version. The whole mystery of Philip Barnes had been upstaged. Ben was glad to have his attention drawn by a hand on his elbow.

It was Carl Zimmerman. "Ben," he said, "Fels and I have to go back with some of the Department people, but could we have a word together at the reception?"

The eulogies had ended and a general seepage toward the black limousines was under way. "Sure, Carl," Ben said, nodding toward Quentin Fels. "I'll go through the receiving line as quick as I can. What about you, Captain? Can I give you a lift?"

But Captain Rigsby announced that his funeral duties were over. He had not been invited to the reception. He was therefore free to go home, change his clothes and take a shower. Safford stifled a wave of envy and turned to the parking lot.

At the Nuevadorian Embassy Señora Montoya received Congressman Safford before the great drawing room.

"On behalf of my fellow members of the House, may I extend condolences for this sad occasion? We regret Señor Olivera's death and we particularly regret that it should have happened in our country."

"Thank you. Manuel will be gravely missed by those who had the privilege of working with him. He was a dedicated public servant."

Safford, who remembered some of the exchanges between

157

Dr. Olivera and Señora Montoya, would have been willing to leave it at that. Señora Montoya had something further to say.

"I see that your young constituent is not with us. Perhaps she was unable to be here?"

"Mrs. Jenks? I didn't know she was invited."

"But certainly. All Sears Scholars who have resided in Nuevador were invited. I myself ordered the invitations sent to Mr. Fels."

Ben said that Mrs. Jenks was probably out of town. But, as he moved on, he was thinking hard. Had Karen decided that a funeral reception in the Nuevadorian Embassy was no place for her? If so, she was showing more sense than Safford was used to. Or had Quentin Fels suppressed her invitation? It was possible. But, most perplexing of all, why had Señora Montoya made a point of inviting Karen Jenks? That business about all Sears Scholars was so much eyewash.

At the buffet Carl Zimmerman was waiting. Safford described his encounter with Señora Montoya.

"That's interesting," said Zimmerman, "very interesting. Ben, the more I go into this Karen Jenks business, the odder it gets. You remember our talk about those faked pictures?"

"My God, that was back in the good old days. I don't remember a thing about it."

"Well, that's what I want to explain. Grab yourself a glass and let's find a quiet corner."

Suiting action to word, Zimmerman led the way to a window niche.

"When you first showed me the original beach pictures of Karen Jenks—the ones somebody used for the doctored photos—I said we'd look into it."

"Yes?"

"And I don't like what we've come up with. In the first place, the store that developed Karen's film was broken into while her negatives were there. Nothing was stolen. But the break-in was reported to the police, and we tracked it down. Then, the first paper to publish pictures of the cathedral incident was the biggest daily in Nuevador. It's pro-American, if anything. But the editors insist that the photographer has disappeared. Nobody knows where he is."

"So, it's as big a mystery as ever," Ben said.

Zimmerman shook his head. "Hell no, it's bigger. The pro-Americans started the hue and cry. The Olivera crowd didn't even try to exploit the situation until Karen was on her way home. They did their best to fan the flames, but, by then, it was too late."

Safford tried to digest this information. "Wait a minute, Carl. Let me get this straight. You're saying the whole cathedral incident was planned after someone had pictures of Karen Jenks. And that the motive was not simply to stir up anti-American feeling."

Carl Zimmerman looked unhappy. "Yes. And, if you knock out a political motive, then you have to look for a corruption motive. Dammit, this whole thing made sense until Olivera got himself murdered!"

"Oh?" Safford did not agree. "If anything makes sense to you, Carl, you're way ahead of me."

"Look at it this way. Karen Jenks yelled corruption in Nuevador, and she got framed. Then she comes up here and yells the same thing to Barnes. And Barnes has his finger on every detail of those shipments. He gets suspicious, starts looking around, and he gets murdered! That makes sense, doesn't it?"

"Except that the GAO has proved nothing was stolen," Safford protested.

Zimmerman did not falter. "Suppose somebody wanted to raise a stink about corruption—even though it didn't exist? What better way to do it than throw Karen out of Nuevador? She was bound to turn up in Washington, screaming corruption. And, Ben, you know that any foreign aid program has its weak spots. TASA would have had them too, if it hadn't been for Phil Barnes."

"You think that's why Barnes was murdered?" Ben asked skeptically.

Zimmerman's enthusiasm collapsed. "Absolutely. Except for one little thing—Olivera's murder."

"And why does that torpedo your theory?"

"Hell, it was Olivera's death that triggered the audit. Since then, everybody's had to wash out the corruption angle."

Ben liked to keep things simple. "Isn't it possible that Olivera was murdered because he knew something about Barnes' death? Even political murderers don't want to be caught."

Before Zimmerman could comment, they were joined by Quentin Fels.

"Don't you think it's all right to leave now?" he asked them. "I'm not up on the protocol, but half an hour should be enough, surely."

"Yes," said Zimmerman, the expert. "Half an hour to forty-five minutes. Oh, by the way, Quentin, are things back to normal at the Sears Foundation?"

"What? Oh, sorry, Carl. I've got to dash," said Fels with a worried look at his watch.

Safford advised him to break away while he could. Fels took the advice. He darted toward the door, ignoring several acquaintances.

"Everybody's getting strange," said Zimmerman reflectively. "I'll bet this is the first time Quentin Fels has been too busy to hang around the Nuevadorian Embassy."

Ben was looking after Fels. "He's certainly in a hurry. There may be more to Quentin Fels' life than you and I know."

A shower, clean clothes and an early supper went far toward improving Ben's outlook. This advantage was wasted, it developed, because when Safford returned to his office that evening, a visitor was waiting for him. Captain Rigsby was almost inarticulate with rage.

"I've been trying to get a hold of you. Your girl didn't know where you were," he snapped. He was standing over Madge Anderson who put down the phone as soon as she saw Ben.

Safford looked inquiringly at her, but replied, "I've been having dinner. At the Mayflower."

"I suppose there are witnesses to that?" Rigsby ground out.

Ben refused to be startled. "About half the Democratic party, Captain," he said. "Now, suppose you tell me what this is all about."

Rigsby let out a long breath. "Sorry, but this thing is getting to me. To think, I had the whole bunch under my eye at the cemetery, and then—"

"Then, what?"

"Late this afternoon, someone beat it out to Maryland and stole Philip Barnes' car, that's what!"

Safford whistled silently.

"You didn't repeat what I told you about that car, did you? Not that there's any reason you shouldn't have," Rigsby added hastily, "but it would be nice to narrow the field."

"I didn't tell anyone, Captain, but I'm afraid you did." Safford reminded the policeman that Howard Creighton had been a step away during their funeral conversation. "And, of course, at the end Carl Zimmerman came up."

"And either one of them could have told someone else," Rigsby said sourly.

But Ben Safford was not listening. He was remembering that Zimmerman had not been alone. Behind him, almost obscured by his muscular hulk, had been the silent shadow of Quentin Fels. A busy man, Quentin Fels. First he hovered

161

by the side of the State Department. Then he hastened away from the Nuevadorian Embassy. And in between, he might be destroying invitations to Karen Jenks.

"And Quentin Fels," he said firmly. "He heard you, too."

Chapter 18

The next morning brought an unexpected development. Ben was at his desk, finishing his review of a committee report, when Congressman Oakes lumbered in.

"I don't want to be a nosy parker," he said, "but someone's got to talk sense to you, Ben."

Ben looked at his visitor with amusement. In a world of increasing hysteria, Oakes remained an unflappable monument to calm.

Yet for all his nonchalance, Eugene Valingham Oakes kept an eye on essentials. So Ben replied:

"What has somebody got to talk to me about?"

Val harrumphed: "This damn Nuevadorian mess."

Ben braced himself.

Val was continuing, "Now Ben, you've got an election to win this fall. None of this publicity is doing you any good back home—I can tell you that."

Val's knowledge of "back home"—wherever it was—was unrivaled. Nor was Ben suspicious of good advice from a member of the Opposition Party. Val was an old friend.

"Lew Frome," Ben said helpfully. "That's my opponent. I don't think he's going to run a very strong race, Val."

Val rumbled his disapproval. "For God's sake, Ben, it doesn't matter one holler in hell what kind of race this Frome runs. You keep popping up in the papers with murders, with stolen cars, with crazy little blondes—and he could run on a laundry ticket and win!"

"I agree with you, Val," said Ben. "There's nothing I'd like better than six weeks of headlines about Congressman Safford and the Agriculture Bill, or Congressman Safford getting federal funds for Newburg—but what the hell! So long as this damned brew is still boiling, it's a lot more dramatic than the price of soybeans. I'm stuck with it."

Val thought deeply.

"Well then," he emerged to say, "you'd better see that it stops boiling."

Congressman Benton Safford was only human, and he had been getting a little too much good advice in recent weeks.

"That's easy enough to say," he pointed out, "but it's a pretty big order. Do you know what happened yesterday?"

Val surprised him. "You mean that car getting stolen? Yup." He observed Ben, then added, "I keep up with things. Can't really help it. Not with Elsie going hog-wild about the whole thing."

"All I need now," said Ben pessimistically, "is a full-scale congressional investigation."

Val weighed this. "The boys wouldn't do it to you—not before the election. And anyway, that GAO investigation was pretty high-powered, and it turned out hunky-dory. No expensive night clubs, no party girls . . ."

"Tony," Ben interrupted to say, "is suspicious about how clean TASA turns out to be. Hell, Val, it's one damned fool thing after another. First Karen Jenks and her wild accusations . . ."

"Now hold it!" Val put up a pudgy hand. "Let's just start at the beginning. I don't say this little pussy is doing you any good—but we might as well start right. Just how wild are her accusations?"

Ben glared at him. "Look, Val, the entire Government Accounting Office has just gone over TASA and the whole damned aid program to Nuevador with a fine-tooth comb. There isn't one penny missing. There isn't one piece of equipment missing! No black market . . ."

Val halted him. "Then why did the girl make the accusations?"

Ben had thought about this. "I don't think she knows herself. If she did, we might not have had two murders."

Again Val Oakes surprised Ben. "You know, I've never met the little lady. I think I'd like to."

Ben opened his mouth, then shut it. An encounter between Karen Kimball Jenks and Eugene Valingham Oakes should be worth seeing.

An hour later, Karen Jenks was on her best behavior.

"Let me recommend the shrimp salad," Val said seriously.

When Karen ordered shrimp salad, he fairly twinkled at her.

In other hands, this courtliness would have sparked the worst in Karen. But Val Oakes was—Ben remembered—a notable charmer, causing temperance ladies and whole Baptist congregations to champion his reprobate cause. One intense young woman was child's play for him. Certainly he got what he wanted. Karen told him the whole sad story of her stay in Nuevador, from the doctored photographs to what she had seen and heard in Montecigalpa. Val listened as if transfixed.

In the midst of her narrative a flash of the old Karen appeared.

"I don't care what that GAO report claims," she said indignantly. "Everybody who saw those thirteen crates of equipment knew they'd end up on the black market. It was an open secret. There's been some sort of cover-up . . ."

"Now, Karen," Ben began mildly, "you don't know the GAO—"

Without giving Ben a chance to finish, Val Oakes said, "Yes, indeed. That's very interesting. Very interesting."

"Why?" asked Karen bluntly. "I've been repeating it over and over, without any results."

Val simply beamed paternally but Ben was realistic. "It produced two murders—or have you forgotten Phil Barnes and Manuel Olivera?" he said.

Karen disliked mysteries she could not unravel.

"Maybe they're not tied together? Maybe it's something else—"

Ben was emphatic. "No, first you make accusations, then the man in charge of TASA shipments is murdered. And after that, the only Nuevadorian who opposed them. Then we have assaults on the Barnes house."

"And yesterday, his car was stolen . . ."

Suddenly a phrase of Karen's rang in Ben's ear, loud and true. Val Oakes and Karen Jenks were talking to each other, but Ben heard nothing. He was pondering certain truths.

Namely, that there were no shortages in the TASA shipments to Nuevador.

But suddenly it occurred to him that other truths were inescapable, even if they did not have the authority of the GAO behind them.

For instance, Karen had been hustled out of Nuevador and discredited for a reason.

Phil Barnes and Manuel Olivera had been murdered for a reason.

For the first time, Ben thought he could see what that reason might be.

He roused himself, to discover that his companions had moved onto a new subject.

". . . look at it this way," Val Oakes was saying with virtuous wickedness. "If you send the little boy to Sunday

166

school, he'll learn all the Bible stories. Believe me, you never can tell when one might not come in handy."

"No," she said simply, "my son isn't going to be brain-washed when he's young. When he's grown up, he can make his own decisions. But I'm not sending him off to be filled with a lot of prejudice . . ."

Val was flatteringly interested in every word. That was the trick, Ben reflected. Karen Jenks disapproved of Val Oakes' politics, public style and personal manner. It didn't matter. After talking to him about herself she became, in her own way, one of his conquests.

". . . and I think that formal religion tends to produce people with closed minds."

Val surveyed his blueberries and chuckled. "I can't deny that some church people can be a little rigid in their thinking."

Karen could not resist. Little did she know, Ben thought, that Val Oakes regularly addressed the South Dakota Methodist Assembly.

". . . rigid! For the last two weeks I've met people who simply can't assimilate any new ideas!"

"Some of your ideas, Karen," said Ben pleasantly, "take a lot of assimilating."

But even as he spoke, he remembered another of Karen's judgments . . . *that sanctimonious little bastard.*

And a brother's praise . . . *a God-fearing man.*

"Well, I don't know what to make of her," said Val Oakes after protracted farewells to Karen. "She can talk up a storm—I see that. But if she's making everything up, I don't see why. No, you're not going to get much help from her."

"Oh I don't know," said Ben thoughtfully as they climbed upstairs, past tourists, photographers and the House guards. "I don't know, Val."

"You got an idea?" Oakes asked, sounding pleased.

"Not really an idea," Ben replied honestly. "Just the beginning of one."

"Hell," said Val Oakes robustly, "that's all you need. I knew that all I had to do was shake you up a little."

With that, he marched off. Watching him, Ben realized that Val Oakes was going to take credit for any clarification to come. Ben did not grudge it to him. If that first glimmer of an idea were right, Val would have earned it.

The first step was a telephone call to Captain Rigsby. Rigsby's voice did not reassure him. Courteous as ever, but very tired.

"Captain," Ben said, "it's just occurred to me that this break-in at Phil Barnes' house—and now the theft of his car—mean that somebody is looking for something."

This was greeted by silence. Then: "It occurred to us, too," said Captain Rigsby without inflection.

Ben pushed on. "I think I may know what it is they're looking for. And also, where it is."

There was a longer silence.

"Why don't you tell me?" said Rigsby.

Ben did.

Half an hour later, Rigsby and Congressman Safford in an unmarked car were speeding north just ahead of the evening rush hour.

Rigsby was excited. "We went over Barnes' office, his house, his car—as well as his safe deposit box. Nothing! Of course, not knowing what we were looking for made things a lot harder."

"What you were looking for," said Ben thoughtfully, "could have been very small. Just a packet of documents—proving Karen Jenks was, in her own way, right. The rest of us, including the GAO, were wrong. That is, if this idea of mine has anything to it."

Rigsby murmured a profanity, then said: "From where I sit, you've got to be right. It's the first thing in this whole damned case that makes any kind of sense."

"Yes," said Ben. "That's what appeals to me. Once you

pull one thread, the whole web comes apart. Karen Jenks saw too much. Philip Barnes knew too much. Olivera? He must have suspected too much."

"Suspected, hell!" Rigsby exclaimed bitterly. "He had proof right under his nose—and so, by God, did I! But I didn't see it until half an hour ago."

They drove on in silence.

The nearer they got to their destination, the less confident Ben Safford became. "Of course, I may be wrong," he said suddenly. "Maybe Barnes didn't leave the papers here. But somebody's already searched his office, his home, and his car—with no luck. And this was the other big interest in Barnes' life."

Rigsby was still kicking himself. "The place," he said, "where Philip Barnes spent every Wednesday night—including the night before he was murdered."

The car had come to a halt before the Garrett Park Calvary Church.

"Where," Rigsby continued, "Phil Barnes conducted the choir. And led choir practice every Wednesday night."

Where, Ben added to himself, there must be a choir room with lockers, with drawers, with shelves.

Rigsby and Ben clambered out and stood looking at the modest red brick building with its sparkling white columns. VISITORS WELCOME, read the small notice. FOR MEDITATION AND PRAYER.

They found the choir room to the left. It was sunny with bright uncurtained windows. Hanging from wooden pegs were fifteen or twenty gowns. Above them, a shelf ran the length of the room, holding hymnals and other personal items. At intervals there were labels with names. Rigsby and Ben circled the room.

"Here it is," said Rigsby.

The label read: *P. Barnes.*

On the shelf above, thrust carelessly atop a pile of music,

was a long manila envelop marked *TASA*. Swiftly Rigsby tilted the contents onto the sun-splashed table.

One look was enough.

"This," said Ben, "is the beginning of the end."

Chapter 19

The next twenty-four hours were productive. Experts from federal agencies made short work of the TASA papers which Rigsby and Safford had found in Philip Barnes' church.

"My God!" said a stunned man from GAO. "My God!"

There was no time to waste. Already coded telephone calls were being placed to Nuevador, to Chicago, to Maryland. And each new piece of information confirmed the broad outlines. By the end of the workday, an ingenious conspiracy had been laid bare in all its detail.

But this did not satisfy Captain Rigsby.

"The trouble with these VIPs," he complained, "is that they're only interested in the big picture. They're not interested in the details—like the fact that there have been two murders in my backyard!"

Benton Safford reminded him that, with the basic plot uncovered, there was no longer any doubt about who the murderer was.

"Sure!" scoffed Rigsby. "But it's evidence I want! And I won't have much chance of getting it once the brass lower the boom. When my man hears how the conspiracy has been blown sky-high, he'll do a flit. He'll be in Switzerland or Mexico in eight hours."

Safford was forced to agree. The governments of Nuevador and the United States planned to move in forty-eight hours; they were more interested in stabilizing the political situation than in convicting the murderer of Philip Barnes and Manuel Olivera.

A thought began to form. "What do you need?" Ben asked.

"I need hard proof tying my guy into the conspiracy. Proof that a jury will understand. Not proof that a certified accountant has to explain!"

Safford leaned forward. "Well, then, Captain," he began, "what about a little trap? Suppose you . . ."

Fifteen minutes later, Captain Rigsby slapped his knee. "That's it! I tip this SOB off to the fact that Barnes left things at the church. Then he'll have to move."

The next day everything went according to plan. At two o'clock, Rigsby made his telephone call, casually inserting a reference to the Garrett Park Calvary Church. At five o'clock, the blue-denimed figure who had been mowing and removing a lawn next to the church reported.

"He bit!" Rigsby was jubilant. "Now we can nab him in the act. It's as simple as ABC!"

At six o'clock the guardhouse at the TASA warehouse in Maryland became conspicuously empty, to remain so for the rest of the evening. At eight, a car swerved past the darkened hut and parked in the shadows at the far end of the lot. The murderer was following Captain Rigsby's timetable.

"We'll give him twenty minutes," Rigsby announced at his field station a quarter of a mile away. "It's a good thing we got everybody out of the warehouse. This guy is dangerous."

At eight-ten Rigsby's strategy suffered its first setback. A second car swept past the guardhouse.

"Now, what the hell!" mumbled a startled federal agent, ducking out of sight. Urgently, he started reporting into a walkie-talkie.

"That's right, Captain. Another one has gone in. It's an old VW, license number . . ."

Also at eight-ten, Doug Travers corrected the last page of a speech, gave it back to Madge and stretched luxuriantly.

"Well, that's that! Is there anything else, sir?"

"No," said Ben. "You two can knock off for the evening. Thanks for staying. Don't bother to lock up, Madge. I'll be here for a while."

In accordance with Captain Rigsby's request for discretion, Ben had not told his staff how the police were closing in on a killer. In return, the Captain had promised to call him as soon as the trap was sprung. Ben did not intend to leave his office before that call came.

Doug was rolling his sleeves down and sliding his tie back into place. "Madge, if it's not out of your way, can you drop me off?" he asked. "Karen has the car."

"Sure," Madge said amiably, taking a soap box and towel from her desk. "I'll be ready in a minute."

Ben was interested to note that his earlier prediction had worked out. He had stayed clear of Doug for a day. Now Doug could make casual references to Karen without embarrassing anybody. Madge, of course, was fully up-to-date.

"Karen left you high and dry for the evening?" Ben asked without much interest.

"Oh, I expect she'll be back early." A reminiscent smile played over Doug's face. "But she left some kind of crazy message with Madge about taking the car."

"She's not mixed up with TASA again, is she?"

Doug was reassuring. "I don't think so. She said something nutty to Madge about having realized that thirteen doesn't make a dozen. Said she was going to track it down."

173

"What?"

Safford had surged out of his chair in one leap. Doug stared at him. "What else did she say?" Ben asked urgently.

"That there was one man who ought to know. He could clear everything up."

"Oh, my God!"

Doug had become infected by Safford's obvious alarm. Now, he too was on his feet.

"But I thought it was something domestic. What's wrong?"

Ben was already striding toward the door. "We've got to get right down there. This is one thing Rigsby doesn't expect. Karen is in danger!"

And as Doug swept past him, he hastily began to explain.

It had, in fact, started as something domestic. Karen had wanted to add a personal touch to Doug's furnished apartment—a touch of gaiety and joy to signify a new life. After shopping she had stepped into a florist's for a dozen carnations. The florist, inspired by Karen's glowing radiance, had been gallant. Unfortunately, the first person Karen met outside was Russ Gallagher.

"Oh, Christ!" he jeered. "Look at our little homemaker, complete with the groceries and a dozen posies."

"Not a dozen," Karen countered. "A baker's dozen. The florist gave me one extra."

As usual, Gallagher was more interested in his own problems than Karen's. "Either there are twelve of them and it's a dozen, or there aren't twelve and it's not a dozen. To hell with all that jazz! Look Karen, you can't cop out now, just because you want to play house with some second-rate Romeo. I've got a guy from *Life* all lined up. It won't take more than a couple of hours . . ."

He started a hard sell. Russ Gallagher had begun to learn that, by himself, he had almost no publicity value. It took Karen ten minutes to get rid of him, and another five to drive back to Doug's apartment. Throughout this interval a single phrase percolated through her mind. *If there are thirteen, it's not a dozen.* She was putting the carnations into water when she summed up her confusion in one sentence:

"There was an extra crate."

She did not know what this fact meant. She did know that it was terribly important. What was the right thing to do with it? Karen remembered harsh words from Ben Safford, from Carl Zimmerman, from Howard Creighton. And, most important of all, from Doug Travers. She would prove she was not a publicity hound like Russ Gallagher. She could act like a responsible adult. She would take her fact to the man who must know what it meant.

Her enthusiasm led her to forget the time. Office hours were over.

"He's gone out to dinner," the phone said. "What's that? Oh, oh yes, he'll be working after dinner. You'd better call back after seven."

Her second call was no more fruitful.

"I don't think he's here," another bored voice said. "Well, yes, I suppose I could look around." There was a long period while Karen listened to the hum of the lines. Finally: "It looks like you're out of luck. His car's not here. He's probably gone to the TASA warehouse in Maryland. You'll have to try again in the morning."

Karen had no intention of waiting until morning. Each passing hour convinced her that she held the key to the mystery in her hand. She asked for directions to the warehouse.

"Mrs. Jenks!" The man jerked his hand back from the file drawer.

They were in a small utilitarian cinderblock entrance hall, lit by a naked bulb. Battered file cabinets stood against the wall.

"Mr. Creighton, I've been trying to get you for hours."
Karen stood in the doorway.

Howard Creighton's voice was almost normal. "And what
do you want from me?"

"It's about the crates, the ones I saw on the docks in
Nuevador. There were thirteen of them!" Karen stepped into
the light.

If Creighton's breathing became more labored, Karen did
not notice. "Don't you see?" she demanded impatiently.
"There should have been only twelve. There was an extra
crate. It could be terribly important."

Creighton pulled the drawer out further. Obviously he
intended to go on with whatever he had been doing. "Oh,
could it?" he asked obscurely.

Karen was stung by his indifference. The words tumbled
out in a stream. "Of course, it could be! You, of all people,
must see that! Why on earth did I come to you? When
you're too wrapped up in that file drawer even to pay
attention. Once I thought of it, I realized it could be the
answer! I don't know exactly how, but surely you can figure
it out—if you're willing to take the trouble!"

Creighton seemed to settle more firmly onto his heels, as
if he had come to a decision. But, Karen thought contemptuously, he was the last man in the world capable of decision. You'd think someone right in TASA would understand . . .

Suddenly her thoughts took a sickening turn. She herself
had said it. Howard Creighton—of all people—should understand. In fact, he should have understood the minute
she opened her mouth, weeks ago, at her first interview.
But he didn't have to understand. He didn't have to figure
anything out. He had known all along.

Then, Karen knew what decision Creighton had just come
to. She had given herself away. He could not let her talk to
anyone else.

Desperately, she tried to think. He stood between her

176

and the entrance. Beyond him was a swinging door, with small diamond windows showing only darkness.

"That door." Karen forced herself to concentrate. "That door is my only chance. If only he looks away . . ."

Just then Howard Creighton found what he was looking for.

"Here it is! At last!"

With both hands, he took out a folder, and started to leaf through it, staring down with blazing eyes. "I knew it," he muttered. "I knew it."

Karen took a deep breath and steeled herself to step forward.

He was intent.

With a wild scramble, she hurled herself against the swinging doors.

They yielded. She stumbled into inky blackness. Fighting every instinct, Karen forced herself onward, running as fast as she could. Behind her, there was one hoarse shout—then nothing.

"Move, move, move!" she told herself, but abruptly she ran into a large object. Momentarily panicked, she flung out terrified arms. Then, moving more carefully, she slid along a barrier in hasty half-steps.

Still there were no sounds behind her.

"Maybe," she told herself shakily. "Maybe . . ."

But at that instant her ankle caught painfully against something. Before she knew what was happening, she was sprawled on a cold concrete floor.

It saved her life, for, simultaneously, a thin string of bulbs near the swinging doors was switched on. Karen raised her head. She was in a huge storage area, she realized. Long rows of crates and metal racks were traversed by narrow corridors.

"Where are you?"

It was almost conversational.

"He can't see me," Karen thought with a sudden surge of hope.

With an effort, she tried to control her ragged breathing. Couldn't he hear that pulsating engine throbbing in her own ears? She waited for a moment, then, with infinite care, moved farther into the sheltering shadow, farther from the lights by the doorway.

"You're not going to get away, you little bitch!"

Footsteps—hurried at first—then slowing. He was going to search up each row, down each row.

Karen bit her lip, when, from the other side of the warehouse, a staccato rustling broke the silence.

"Ha!" Howard Creighton was triumphant.

Dimly, Karen saw him—a black shadow, rushing past her hiding place. Scarcely breathing, she raised herself to her hands and knees. There had to be some way out of this maze that did not lead her back to that dangerous ribbon of light.

Suddenly, a scurry of sound nearby made her start.

Bright eyes in the darkness—gone even as she looked. "A cat," she said to herself. Perhaps it was a cat who had decoyed the hunter away from her.

As if in reply, there was a distant cry, frightened and frightening.

"Where are you? You can't hide here all night!" The voice was rising uncontrollably.

And there was more noise. He was running aimlessly up and down long rows, pushing aside boxes, swearing aloud. He was making too much noise himself to hear her, Karen knew. This was her chance.

Karen rose and took three steps. She moved swiftly, silently. But swiftness was her undoing. She did not see the small wheeled trolley in her path. The next moment she had fallen to the ground. There was a short, clattering crash.

The cavernous building seemed to take the sound, and echo it from wall to wall. Dazed, Karen struggled to her feet.

There were crashes from her right, her left, from everywhere. One of them was Howard Creighton, now silent—poised for the kill.

At the sound of a footfall Karen spun around. But she had been deceived by the echoes. When Creighton seized her in his stocky powerful arms, he came from behind. She could feel his ragged, warm breath on the nape of her neck. She tried to kick backwards. His dull, murmuring voice hoarsely intoned the same phrase over and over again:

"Little bitch, little bitch . . ."

Then he heaved her off her feet, and she knew her last hope of defending herself was gone. Frantically she twisted her head.

At that moment the overhead flood lights came on.

In horror, she stared directly into the inhuman mask that had once been Howard Creighton's face. Then instinct took over. She wildly averted her eyes to stare over his shoulder.

That can't be Doug, she thought. That can't be Doug.

"Creighton!"

Doug Travers' bull-like roar let loose a tumultuous resonance that was picked up in the noise made by other advancing men.

Almost sobbing, Creighton put all his strength into throwing Karen aside. Then he turned to face his assailant. Karen gave a cry of pain as she was hurled against a heavy shrouded object looming in the dark. She saw Doug and Creighton charge each other; her cry changed into a scream of warning that welled from deep within her.

Then it was as if all light were extinguished again. Karen felt herself falling into a black, bottomless pit.

Chapter 20

"Then, since it was Howard Creighton, I was right all along!"

It was three days later and Karen Jenks, predictably enough, was jumping to conclusions.

"No, you weren't," Safford said severely. "You took a U-turn. What's more, you got the rest of us haring off in the wrong direction."

Before Karen could protest, Doug Travers intervened. "We've been out of things these last few days, sir. We never did hear any of the explanations."

The young people had been busy with their own affairs. After the capture of Howard Creighton, Doug Travers had sped off after Karen's ambulance. Now Safford was giving them lunch to celebrate their engagement.

As he looked at his guests across the table, Ben decided that his administrative assistant, although undoubtedly crazy, had more self-possession than most men twenty years older. Because Karen had recovered from her struggles with Howard Creighton in the TASA warehouse. She could have been reclining in a hospital bed, wrapped in a soft little jacket. She could have entered the restaurant on Doug's arm, looking pale and fragile. Instead she had come bouncing in, full of vigor, with the left side of her face flaunting a fruity black eye. The disfigurement looked authentically home-brewed. Did Doug Travers realize that every cab driver, every waiter, every elevator operator assumed he had belted the lady? Or did he go one step further and realize that, after five minutes' exposure to Karen, they were all on his side?

"But what was Creighton trying to hide," Doug persisted, "if there weren't any shortages?"

"He was trying to hide the fact that there was too much in TASA's warehouse—not too little."

"Well, that's a new wrinkle," Doug admitted. "You mean to say you figured that out?"

Safford took the time to refill their champagne glasses while he cast his mind back. "It wasn't so hard if you skipped the distractions. It suddenly came to me that I'd been hearing two things, over and over again. First, of course, was Karen describing thirteen crates, each as big as a room and filled with TASA aid, lying on the dock in Nuevador. She said it so often, and so loud and clear, that I almost overlooked the fact that everybody else was saying each TASA shipment consisted of twelve crates."

Karen objected. "But that simply doesn't make sense!"

"Never mind whether it makes sense or not," he directed. "Just remember it means something was being *added* to the regular TASA shipment. The other refrain started after Philip Barnes was pushed out the window. People kept telling us that the current shipment to Nuevador was being delayed because of his death. Which brings us to Philip Barnes, the first murder victim, a man about whom we know almost nothing."

"Except that he was the work horse over at TASA. The man who knew all the details," prompted Doug, "and the man who might be alerted by Karen's story."

181

Ben snorted politely. "That's what we were supposed to think. But does it ring true? If he was on top of all that detail, why did he need Karen to tip him off? Assume something illicit was being added to the Nuevador shipments. Then Philip Barnes appears in a different light. He was the ideal man to accomplish it. He checked deliveries, he sent things back to the warehouse until he had each shipment the way he wanted it, he controlled the files."

"I suppose so." Doug was nodding reluctant agreement. "But he sounded like such a model civil service employee."

"I think Phil Barnes was a holier-than-thou type," Ben said, to keep from hearing Karen's way of putting it. "He was a model civil servant and, like most of them, he didn't get paid enough. Rigsby's run down a lot of big expenditures in the Barnes household—from new heating systems to new cars—that weren't coming out of Barnes' salary. He was taking a pay-off . . ."

"For adding something to the TASA shipments," Doug mused. "I can make a good guess at what that something was."

"I forgot you left before we pried open the crate that Howard Creighton was marking. It was filled with machine guns, automatic rifles and hand grenades."

"Gun running!" Karen Jenks' eyes glowed.

She looked so vivacious that Ben examined her closely for the first time. His worst fears were confirmed. The outrageous little minx had not tried to play down her black eye. Instead she was deliberately playing it up. She had used a blue-purple eye shadow on her good eye and the same color was reflected in the vivid silk shift she wore. Reluctantly he had to admit that she knew what she was doing. The net result was attractive and compelling. He had a dim suspicion that the desire roused was mildly perverse. Like a longing to take a good healthy sock at the other eye. What's more, the girl was well aware of this effect.

His inspection had not gone unnoticed. Karen grinned at him provocatively.

"Yes, smuggling arms," he said. "You both know the situation in Nuevador. The Montoya crowd wasn't thinking of a drawn-out civil war. All they needed was a good sharp uprising, with arms apparently supplied by the United States. They would have had the army on their side within forty-eight hours."

"That's some audit they had at TASA," Karen scoffed. "If it overlooked a stockpile of weapons."

"No, you're not being fair to the GAO. TASA's warehouse held material to be sent to Brazil and Argentina and every other Latin American country. The GAO wasn't asked to check that inventory. They were asked to prove that the aid already sent to Nuevador had actually gotten to the right place. I don't think any ordinary government check would have caught Creighton. The real controls at TASA are on the money they spend and on the ultimate arrival of their equipment."

Karen was accusing. "I don't understand that."

"I should have listened to Manuel Olivera. He had the right idea about you." Safford grinned at her. "He said that you saw things all right, but that you reacted emotionally. In other words, that your observation was accurate, but that your judgment was terrible. It would have saved us all a lot of trouble."

"I suppose you're going to explain that," said Karen stiffly.

"Sure. Philip Barnes, bribed by Howard Creighton, was letting guns into the TASA warehouse. They came in phony packaging like standard agricultural equipment. Since he paid no money for these deliveries, he could suppress the delivery documents. Then, once a month, he assembled a shipment for Nuevador—eleven crates of genuine agricultural equipment and one crate of small arms. These twelve crates were closed with the TASA seal. Therefore they were not examined either by the export controls of the United States or the import controls of Nuevador. They were still sealed when they ended up on the dock where you saw them."

"But, sir—" began Doug.

"I know, I know," Ben cut him off. "You're going to say that the U.S. aid shipment was short. That's where the thirteenth crate comes in. Once the shipment reached Nuevador, the Montoyas had to add a crate of agricultural equipment and, of course, remove the weapons. For a brief period of time there would be thirteen crates. Karen's trip to the docks coincided with one of those periods. Then, she started telling everyone in sight about those thirteen crates and the Montoya agents got scared. They decided to get her out of the country fast. They set up the cathedral incident and Señora Montoya immediately got busy demanding Karen's recall. Her pro-American reputation gave her the ideal excuse for wanting to hush things up as fast as possible."

"That bitch," said Karen darkly. "I might have known she was behind it all."

Doug asserted his authority. "Never mind about the bitch. I want to know about Manuel Olivera. Why was he killed? Had he cottoned on to all this?"

"We'll never know, but he was close enough to terrify Creighton. Remember the meeting we had the afternoon he was killed? Karen was sounding off and Olivera already had the details on TASA shipments. Right there, if he had known it, he could have blown the conspiracy apart."

"Why?" Doug asked.

"Because he had a list of Señora Montoya's imports, too. I didn't understand at first, but I haven't been poring over those lists with a magnifying glass. As soon as I mentioned the thirteenth crate to Captain Rigsby, he was on to it, like a shark. Every single item that Señora Montoya imported for her estancia was not only on a TASA list, but it was imported into Nuevador in the same month! The extra crate was coming in every month as a personal order on her part."

"See?" said Karen irrepressibly. "She was at the back of the whole thing. I wouldn't be surprised if she murdered Olivera."

Safford shook his head. "No. She wasn't risking enough to make murder worthwhile. All she had to worry about, was staying out of Nuevador if the lid came off. Quite apart from the fact that she's a rich woman. Creighton was on the firing line. He had been paid—at a really extraordinary rate—by Señora Montoya to set the whole thing up. In turn, he corrupted Philip Barnes. Barnes was just as good at handling the details for the conspiracy as he was at his legitimate work. But he wanted some insurance. When Karen blew into town, Philip Barnes decided to retire. He scared easily. He told Creighton he was through. Creighton said that was impossible, they were all in it together. But Barnes had a file listing all the illegal weapons deliveries plus photostats of checks from Creighton. Creighton didn't like the sound of that file at all. Then to top things off, Barnes turned up at the Sears Foundation, hysterically talking about repentance. Creighton saw he might crack under pressure; so Creighton took the only sure way of protecting the future. He clubbed Barnes with a marble bookend and tipped him out the window. He must have been desperate to do it."

Doug frowned in thought. "And all this running around since has been Creighton's attempt to find that incriminating file?"

"As a matter of fact, no. Once he assured himself that it wasn't going to turn up at TASA, it didn't bother him much. At any rate that's what he said in his confession, and he seems to be telling the truth. What he overlooked was that Barnes had also secreted the identifying numbers on the crates containing arms. With Barnes dead, Creighton had hundreds of machine guns sitting in the TASA ware-

185

house and couldn't locate them because they were carefully disguised as tractors or something. That's why he ran around searching Barnes' house and car. And that's why the current Nuevador shipment had to be delayed. Of course, once we found the file in Barnes' church, it was a cinch to rig a trap."

"You mean you just gave him a tip as to where he could find the identifying numbers."

"That's right. Naturally Rigsby hung on to everything else. Once Creighton had the numbers, the police simply sent men into the warehouse that night to wait for him. That way, he was caught in the act marking the machine guns for immediate shipment. Once Rigsby knew who the murderer was, he was able to find a witness who placed Creighton in Olivera's elevator at the critical time. When Howard Creighton saw the evidence piling up, he broke down and confessed. In fact, everything went according to plan, except for Karen's arrival."

Safford broke off to look indulgently at his guests. Karen Jenks was as singleminded as ever.

"And Señora Montoya? Does she get off scot-free?"

"There's nothing wrong with that lady's grapevine. At seven o'clock on the morning after Creighton's arrest, she was aboard a jet to Paris. It turns out that the whole Montoya family has been sitting around, poised for flight. The children went to Europe the day after Barnes was killed. And Señor Montoya, who was running the show in Nuevador, took a business trip to Venezuela. He's been sitting there, ready to go back home and have his uprising or, alternatively, to go to Europe. I expect he's already in Paris."

"Won't the Nuevadorian Government try to get them back?" asked Karen indignantly.

"I doubt it. Carl Zimmerman has flown down to Nuevador to talk things out with their ministers. But they're as anxious as we are to softpedal the whole business. I think

Creighton is going to be persuaded to plead guilty. There will be a very fast, clean trial without a lot of details. Naturally, I have insisted Karen should be completely exonerated in the process."

Karen shrugged. "I've got other fish to fry," she said elaborately indifferent.

Doug grinned. "Karen's sore," he explained. "But I say, now that she's gone this far with her doctorate, she may as well go on. Anyway, I'm beginning to like the idea of being married to a cultural anthropologist."

"A lot you know about it," Karen challenged.

"I know one thing," Doug told her firmly, "you need practice for seeing things through. You don't get rid of me as easily as you did your last husband."

Ben hastily dived into the wine cooler, but when he emerged, prepared to kill the bottle, Karen was not only smiling, she had raised the back of Doug's hand to her cheek.

"Exactly what," asked Ben, "does finishing the doctorate entail?"

"Karen's changed her thesis. Now it's going to be a comparison of Indians in Nuevador with Indians in the United States. She's going to spend a long summer in Arizona. Then, after I've seen you through the election, sir, we'll settle down in Newburg. I can start taking sights on the State Assembly and Karen might think about teaching at the University."

"Or Karen might think about starting other things," said his fiancée.

"Oh, there are lots of possibilities," Doug agreed pleasantly. "Starting with getting married this Friday."

And then the conversation turned to the forthcoming ceremony. Mr. and Mrs. Kimball would be flying up for the occasion. The Safford office would turn out in full force. Maureen would lead an anti-Gallagher faction from C Street. When Ben waved his guests off, he was mildly surprised at the turn of events. He was brought back to reality by a voice at his side.

"Well, Ben, I hear you've got your troubles just about settled," said Val Oakes in mournful congratulation.

"That's right, Val." There was no point in asking which of Oakes' many listening posts had reported.

"And the girl?" Oakes nodded in the wake of the departing cab. "Getting rid of her, too?"

"In a way."

Ben explained about the engagement. Then he described the summer arrangements planned by the Travers couple.

"That boy's got a real head on his shoulders," Val commented. "Keeping her out of the way until after your election, I see."

"I don't think—" Ben began, before pausing for thought. "Good God, I'll bet you're right, Val! That's probably exactly what he has in mind."

Val nodded in ponderous approval.

Ben was amused. "That's all very well, but he's planning a political career himself, you know. How will he fit Karen into that?"

"Cross your bridges when you come to them. She may not be such a problem by then." Oakes was judicious. "But I'll tell you one thing. If he can handle her, that boy's going a long way."

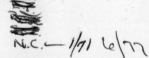